"Rarely can we witness literature like this."

MIGUEL ÁNGEL ÁNGELES, *ROLLING STONE*

"A complex yet magnificent book, solid and slippery at the same time, with poetry that blows one's mind. A great novel."

LA REPUBBLICA

"I don't know how to tell you this but you must get your hands on this novel. Read it as if time didn't matter, in a remote and solitary place, and do not dare to give your copy away as a gift. And finally, may it not be a surprise if it leaves you in unrest and reminds you of something ancient and afar."

RICARDO BAIXERAS, *EL PERIÓDICO*

"One of the most ambitious achievements in the last decade of Mexican literature."

JAIME MESA, *LADO B*

THE ARID SKY

EMILIANO MONGE

THE ARID SKY

Translated from the Spanish by
Thomas Bunstead

RESTLESS BOOKS
BROOKLYN, NEW YORK

Esta publicación fue realizada con el estímulo del Programa de Apoyo a la
Traducción (PROTRAD) dependiente de instituciones culturales mexicanas.

This publication was realized with the assistance of the Programa de Apoyo
a la Traducción (PROTRAD), dependent on Mexican cultural institutions.

First Restless Books paperback edition August 2018

Paperback ISBN: 9781632061348
Library of Congress Control Number: 2016940789

Cover design by Greg Mortimer
Set in Garibaldi by Tetragon, London
Printed in Canada

1 3 5 7 9 10 8 6 4 2

Restless Books, Inc.
232 3rd Street, Suite A111
Brooklyn, NY 11215

www.restlessbooks.org
publisher@restlessbooks.org

To Damián García Vázquez

CONTENTS

I am one, my liege,
Whom the vile blows and buffets of the world
Have so incensed that I am reckless what
I do to spite the world.

SHAKESPEARE, *MACBETH*

THE ARID SKY

LEAVING

THIS IS THE STORY of a man who, though he did not know it, was the era in which he lived, and of a place itself held within that man's name: Germán Alcántara Carnero. A story of violence both inevitable and boundless, one that demands to be told as biography, though not in any kind of sequence, and that should in no way have begun here: May 13, 1956, as the sun inches closer to its noonday position, the time of day when women lower the blinds in their houses, birds shelter in the recesses of limewashed walls or in the branches of the trees recently back in leaf, and the scattered cacti gather their shadows close like shawls. A moment in which Germán Alcántara Carnero, first and only son to Félix Salvador Germán Alcántara Arreola and María del Pilar y del Consuelo Carnero

3

Villalobos, sits in his office, a bare and comfortless room, and considers these present minutes as though considering the map of his life. A moment he has imagined so many times he cannot believe it has finally come to pass.

Done, thinks Germán Alcántara Carnero, *finally I am done*, at which scores of emotions beat and flutter inside him, as birds beat and flutter their wings when taking to the air. *Not a moment too soon*, he says to himself, this man we have just now met. *On this side*, he says, tracing a line across his desk, *on this side I place the life I have led, and on this my life to come. Here stay the anger, the hatred, the sadness, and there, over there lie hope—there lies all solace*. Suddenly shaking his head and clapping his hands together, Germán Alcántara Carnero—whom we are due to follow throughout this story, a story that nonetheless need not unfold linearly given that first of all, before this telling, it was a life, and in a life the only matter are the moments that shine brightly—sweeps away the imaginary line and, noticing a small scrap of tin on one side, straightaway becomes lost in a vision, a prospect of a shack with two women standing in the doorway, only for that vision to disappear in a second: there, a heat-drunken fly has collided with his face. The scrap of tin, his since he was a child, ceases to be a shack with two women in the doorway and becomes just an object once more—just an object.

The fly completes a circuit of the room before coming to land on a heavy contraption to one side of him: a gray desk fan, the blades of which have long since lain motionless. Under the layer of dust the fan, which Germán Alcántara Carnero should have discarded long ago, is yellow. But he has never been able to do it, to throw away the gift he was given by Anne Lucretius Ford the first time she came to see him here at the office. The gray broken-down fan prompts the memory in this man—whom as we progress we will also call *ourman*—of turning on his heels in the downstairs passageway once, long ago, and looking up to find Anne Lucretius Ford climbing the stairs, carrying the yellow contraption that he will not, will not be taking with him today. "You have no place in my life now," declares Germán Alcántara Carnero, looking at the three rusty blades but addressing Anne Lucretius Ford: "No place at all!" And, with a brisk shake of his head, the fan turns back into a fan.

"Today I begin anew," declares ourman, as loud as he can. Shaking his head, throwing it from side to side, he insists: "No more thinking about the past. Today, every-thing begins anew." It takes a short while for him to stop shaking his head; he stops only once he feels sure the memories have ceased. It is a moment he has longed for above all else. Another fly, however, crosses his line of vision, drawing his eye over to the portrait on the wall of Teobaldo Pascua Gómez, his former boss, the nose, the craggy cheekbones, the two massifs of his temples, curly eyebrows, lank hair, foreshortened chin, and that cold, barren gaze—ourman cannot help but think: *Yes, I am right to be leaving . . . to stay would only mean ending up like you, that morning, the morning we burned down the church*. Luckily for ourman, the fly pitches into the air again, and he notices he's been swept under once more, that he's allowed memory to drag him down. Germán Alcántara Carnero lifts his gaze away from the portrait of Teobaldo, balls up his fists, reprimands himself—*no more, no more of any of this*—before scanning the oppo-site wall and the objects hanging on it: a pair of thick ropes, three chains, six metal hasps, a handsaw, and various implements of dentistry. He smiles, his first smile in months, again telling himself: "Now, at noon on May 13, 1956, when the sun is at its highest and all the shadows in the world go out, I hereby leave it behind, leave all those people whose breath I cut short, so that I might one day breathe life into another." His smile grows wider as he sends out a laugh, sonorous and deep. Then, slamming both hands down on the desk, gigantic sinewy paws that look to have been fashioned expressly to strangle, maim, and dismember, Germán Alcántara Carnero bisects the cold silence hanging in the air, just as this present moment bisects his very life: "From now on, I'll be the one to decide . . . I'll be more than I have yet been able to be."

"It's come! It's truly come!" says Germán Alcántara Carnero, glancing at the gold-colored door handle: "Yes, forget it all, every single moment spent in this place."

To the benefit of this story's progression, a story best not associated with this idea, *progression*, since it is a story more of leaps and gaps than of sequence, even if our man really were to forget all the time he spent in this accursed place, even if he could, I am here, and I will not forget. I have in my possession certain things he has written, testimonies from five of his men, and some newspaper cuttings—sufficient material to piece together the trail of destruction he left behind. This story, which, as I have said, should not be associated with any chronological thing, is a gallery of moments, and it is a capturing both of the topography of this land and the contours of this era: Germán Alcántara Carnero.

"Go down those stairs now, and never think of any of this again." Upon which ourman tears his eyes away from the door handle as a butcher tears the pelts off animals, and, pushing back his chair, adds: "Go down the hallway, all the way down, don't stop at the ministry room, no goodbyes, no farewells." Heart full, spirit full, Germán Alcántara Carnero, a man so thin it makes you want to touch him just to see if your hand passes clean through, readies himself, pushing back his chair a fraction farther, and in the instant, the very instant of leaving, stops and shouts, in hope that someone might be listening: "You all better not have any surprises lined up. I was clear as clear: no farewells!" Getting up, ourman lets a smile appear on his lips again—*No fond farewell to these things either, none of that*—as he peers grinning around at the many objects piled up inside his office: sorry disused piles of long-neglected objects. "Leave it all behind . . . though perhaps, just perhaps . . . perhaps just the odd thing or two . . . but what do I want a rickety armchair

8

for . . . maybe the filing cabinet, though . . . what use could you possibly have for either! . . . maybe the clock, though, maybe the chain . . . "

"No, just take the *important* things," ourman says, and, after a pause, steps back inside the room, leans down and picks up a crate he brought in yesterday—the significance of this crate being that ourman must already have decided to both leave and to take one or two things along. Ourman drops in a couple of envelopes, some keys tied together with ribbon, the handkerchief he took from the dead body of El Demónico Camilo Mónico Macías Osorio, the sash worn by Anne Lucretius Ford the day she died, the stone he believes to contain a fossil, and a small bundle of fabric that swaddles his lucky charm: the bullet that almost twelve years ago parted his breastbone, came out through the top of his lung, and lodged in his right shoulder blade. And something then tells him that this is as good a moment as any to look inside the bundle, a bundle he has not looked inside in years.

With the bundle open flowerlike before him, Germán Alcántara Carnero, whose smiling mouth is suddenly atwitch, removes the projectile, holds it between forefinger and thumb, and, though he knows very well this is a path better left untaken, nonetheless travels back to the day he was hit. He and his men had surrounded a group hiding out at the dam, when, on some inexplicable impulse, ourman broke cover and shouted: "Come out of there right now! I come alone, can't you see? And I'm waiting."

Bringing his hand up to his chest, he shakes his head once more, that is to say throws it from side to side: he has stumbled into his past again. *Maybe don't take anything, maybe not even the bullet.* And, with a last shake of the head, the memory goes scuttering off. "Leave, leave empty-handed, that way you might one day become *full* again. But what if you forget why you left in the first place? What if you begin to want this all again one day?" To which ourman immediately responds: "Take only the things that will remind you of why you left—the bullet, the handkerchief with Macías's blood all over it, the sash Anne was wearing that day—the day I failed to keep her safe . . . " A jolt, no, a spasm: Ourman hiding in a ditch, his breath constricted, his heartbeats galloping one after the other, his tongue rag-dry, and a couple of his fingers lodged in the bloody wound through which Anne's viscera were spilling. Speaking in a very low voice, all but whispering, and bringing his face in close to hers, he says: "It isn't as bad as you think . . . stop guzzling air like that, would you . . . try breathing a little calmer now." Her knees buckle, and as she hits the ground her eyes close and her mouth opens, and some words come out, words we do not hear for now—though later on we will—because ourman has decided that although he needs to go away from this place armed with certain memories, he would do well not to go wandering about in the dark and snag them now. Two more items go into the crate: the totem he stole from the Prieto Hernández family the night they got their hands on Ignacio del Sagrado Sandoval-Íñiguez Martínez, and a coin he's kept as a memento of the time he lived abroad.

"What has been, will be," ourman mutters as his eyes come to rest on the door handle once more. It makes no sense, what he has just said, and he knows it—just as he also knows that it will always be like this, memories rearing up suddenly, surfacing just when he thinks he's dealt with them for good. *At least the guilt won't be with you . . . now that you're on your way, now that pardon and solace are coming down down down . . . now that you're nearly all and completely gone.* Looking up, his eyes begin to wander once more, oh he lets them. *What does it matter if you are forever remembering, if this keeps on coming back? What matters is that you're leaving.* Smiling, feeling the sun on his face, the big burning bully now past its noonday locus and pounding in through his window, Germán Alcántara Carnero cries out: "What matters is that I'm leaving and I'll never come back!"

Hefting the crate, he decides, *no more—yes, no more thinking about the past, no more of anything that might sully or soil this moment, the setting forth of a story that should not have set forth here*: May 13, 1956, when the heat of the day is overwhelming, the sun having but moments before given up that pivot point in its empire the sky and the insects all and everywhere asleep, Germán Alcántara Carnero, also known as El Gringo, a name his men gave to him long ago, only very briefly worries at his reasons for leaving, takes out the pendulum formed by the bullet that was once lodged inside of him, together with the chain that once belonged to Ignacio del Sagrado Sandoval-Íñiguez Martínez, wraps the chain about his pinky, and watches as the trinket swings back and forth.

"Gotta go," ourman says, and this time his words are unstoppable, they are red-hot seething lava gushing out, and even as they do he unwraps the chain, and in so doing one of his fingertips brushes the old spiderlike scar etched on his sternum. It is nearly as hot now inside the office as it is outside, the kind of heat that no sooner does it touch a thing than that thing is crushed and then distilled: the ground gives off the smell of wood, the jacket on the back of the chair gives off the odor of the leather of which it is made, and the iron trunk reeks of the cold metal it once was. Seconds pass, one or two. The bullet, swinging back and forth from the left hand of Germán Alcántara Carnero, knocks against the spot it sundered many years before, and sends a shudder across his skin.

A smile returns to the face of ourman—whom we will also call El Gringo, this being an alias he likes, for it brings to mind Will D. Glover, an old compeer of his, once very dear—we will come back to Will—a smile and a glimmer in his eyes, a glimmer bright like the crack running the breadth of the window as the sun beats down on the high mesa outside: this current hour is the worst for the heat, when the light is thin and all metal surfaces are aglow as though lit from within. On the bidding of the window's angry cracks, which say to ourman that he should have left by now, he exclaims: "I have to get up, get this over with": he is on the point of leaving the throne, this kingdom and empire he has ruled for almost thirty years. Coiling up the trinket and placing it once more inside its little fabric sheath, El Gringo Alcántara Carnero stretches out both legs and both arms, arches his back, and reverses the chair, hitting the wall behind him and knocking out a thumbtack that held in place the corner of a large map that depicts the local environs, and which, freed of the thumbtack, comes loose, rolling up like an eyelash.

Up on his feet again, ourman takes down the charred wooden Christ he stole—he prefers to say "abducted"— from the church he and his men burned down, a con-flagration we will also come back to, and, placing it in the now nearly full crate, wonders why he wants to keep this idol, which still does not fully belong to him, but one day will, a day we will visit together when the time is such. No, the idol does not belong to ourman on this hottest of days in this sun-blasted place, a place where the wells regularly run dry: the only water source on this high mesa being a dam built long ago that waters the six towns and fifteen slums that pertain to the empire governed by the small ministry from which El Gringo Alcántara Carnero today absconds. An empire that is home to 30,234 inhabitants, the children and grand-children and great-grandchildren, to a one, of incest—men and woman whose veins course with the same courage, aloofness, fears, servility, hatefulness, and guile as did those of the people who settled these lands over the centuries—the same courage, aloofness, fears, servility, hatefulness, and guile, that is, of the few indigenous people who managed to avoid extermination.

When he bends down to pick up the other crate he brought with him, ourman realizes that his back is dripping wet, and says, annoyed: "Not a day for shirts." Tongue out, he sighs, feeling a sudden cramp just above the scar of Baldomero Díaz Cervantes's gunshot. *That burning sensation took its time to go, and now I'm left with this fucking searing cold instead*, thinks El Gringo Alcántara Carnero, moving his chair to one side and tearing down the map of his empire, and then the newspaper cuttings also tacked to the wall, and finally the photograph of a trio of running dogs that he cut out of a magazine one day because it reminded him of the dogs he had as a boy, dogs that came with him the day he left home. The memory of his dogs drags Germán Alcántara Carnero off course, but another chest spasm brings him back. "Like an ice cube onto hot coals," as he once described the sensation to a doctor one day, when the man asked what the matter was. Ourman sees this foreign doctor in his memory and smiles to remember his accent, the strange utensils he produced, and the even stranger way in which he checked his sternum and shoulder blade. Then, going over to the window, ourman lifts his mind back up, focusing on what's important: this long-overdue moment.

In the stunning rust-colored sky—also slightly ocher in color at this time of year due to the great amounts of dust hanging in the air—Germán Alcántara Carnero sees the sun inching farther away from its noontime post and shadows beginning to emerge on the ground. The world is awash with light, and ourman squints, taking in the nearest portion of the town square, his eye then traveling up beyond the treetops and church tower, up at the graves that scatter the mountainside. It would be within his power to list every name etched on those tombstones in the distance, but he knows there's no need, and he wishes there won't ever be again, for that would mean making a roll call of his victims, the victims of the fury that once was in him. "This thing unfurling before me is freedom," he says, not yet knowing that a man may leave a place behind but never his history. It will be many years before he understands: that a man may escape his life but never his shadow.

A peculiar thought, the one that allows ourman to hope, that lets him think he is in a position to put an end to the hatred inside him. A strange calculation, this one, as even now, even as his guilt continues to move him, he considers it a thing that may fade. Like a bird arcing through the sky, full of incomprehension for the laws governing the winds that buffet it, full of hope.

"What has been, will be," ourman will say over and over on the day he dies, the day our story will end, but that is a long way off yet, not yet important. The same goes for his past and future. And for the moment in which ourman was born, and the moment his father died, and all the years he spent in the army and in foreign lands. What matters now is that, finally and without any further intervention of any further memories, the moment of our story's beginning is upon us:

May 13, 1956: El Gringo Alcántara Carnero, raising up his left arm and letting the blinds rattle shut, leaves in thick darkness the office in which we find ourselves. He does not need to see in order to move around the murkiness he has created, he knows it well, every inch of this space and of its neglected heaps of furniture, their scores and scuffs on top and their undersides gobbed and gibbed with his own snot. He grabs his jacket—taken years ago from the first man he ever stuffed in his iron trunk and left to die—from the back of a broken chair. "Time's the killer, not I," he would always say before putting men in his truck. Then, laughing: "Why don't you tell your god to come get you out? Tell him to pull off a little lovely miracle for you." This always made him laugh.

But nor is it the moment for these things! The only thing that matters is that ourman has folded his jacket with unusual attentiveness, placed it over his forearm, turned his body, started to walk toward the door, and is now crossing the threshold, leaving the door open behind him.

El Gringo Alcántara Carnero walks steadily along the hallway, past a couple of overflowing trashcans and a corkboard that spits at him with the black and white likenesses of all the men who have escaped his fury. *They no longer exist*, ourman swears to himself as he comes to the staircase that takes him down to the ground floor, where his arrival makes people look but then look away.

From now on they are nothing, he thinks, finding the emptiness these words produce in him strange, as if something had dropped away from his body, as if he himself were about to take to the air. *They're nothing*. As though to stop feeding the anger would in fact make his existence less heavy, as though solace were out there just waiting for him in the street.

Just as he is about to set foot in the ministry's main room, the scene of his earliest involvement in this line of work, one he entered after coming back from abroad, the country he went away to with El Demónico Macías and returned from in the company of Anne Lucretius Ford and Will D. Glover—a moment for later in our story—his face warps until a look of near-happiness appears, reflecting the cautious joy that for a couple of hours now has slowly been taking hold of his soul.

Pretending to himself he is thirsty, Alcántara Carnero takes one of the paper cones from next to the small fountain and fills it. He drinks from the paper cone, wondering what he'll do with it afterwards. (He'll crumple it up and put it in his pocket.) He wishes to draw the moment out, to savor it. Truly believing that solace is out there, waiting, on the street.

Water drips from the bunched-up paper cone, trickling over ourman's leg and running down it. A couple of steps shy of the ministry room, he hears clapping break out: Will D. Glover whistling with two fingers in his mouth, Óscar el Chino López Ley howling, La Madrina yelling, José Ángel el Cerebro Ordóñez Sánchez pounding on a trashcan as if it were a drum, Ramiro la Madrina López Palas tossing into the air the strips of paper he spent half the morning tearing up, and the Pascua de Ramones twins, Ausencia and Amparo, goading the others, stirring the room. This racket serves to fan the embers of Germán Alcántara Carnero's fury. *I said I wanted to go quietly. I won't let them ruin it now*, he thinks, muttering with eyes narrowed: "To accept praise is to be in people's debt." He narrows his eyes, and yet the vision he wishes to escape, the faces of these applauding men and women, fragments and clinging scraps of their likenesses, accompany him into the darkness.

"Didn't I say no send-off?" He throws his arms wide, he implores. "My fault, of course, thinking they had it in them to follow an order! All the times they've shown that to be absolutely not the case! All the times they've shown they understand precisely fuck all." A couple of steps from the front door, that final borderline between ministry interior and street, Germán Alcántara Carnero stops and spins on his heels with a flourish, and is confronted with a row of silent faces, these now-silent men and women. They are watching him leave. "Let's just see how you all manage now," he grins, hair and shoulders lit golden yellow as the sun breaks through the skylight that broke in the earthquake of February 22, 1946, a day that, unlike the days mentioned heretofore, sheds no light on the life of ourman, and therefore does not form part of our story. "Let's just see how you fuckers manage without me."

"I don't care. Their problem now." With the same forefinger that a moment ago touched the spider of a scar on his chest, ourman loosens the strap on his belt and grips the cold steel he's reached for so many times in his life. *They won't dare pick it up. They haven't got the balls.* Unhurriedly, Germán Alcántara Carnero unholsters the gun, feeling its worn hilt and the weight of the cylinder and the chamber. "I doubt they'll dare while I'm standing here before them." The silence expands like a balloon as he arcs his arm and lets go, launching the weapon into the air, watching as it hits a chair, bounces off the seat, falls to the floor with a clatter. "There's so much stuff up there," he says, looking at them. "If this isn't enough, maybe all those things up there will do." At this, a shudder passes through the people watching him.

"Lot of rage and fury up in my office, too, whoever wants that, plus all the guilt, eh?" He turns on his heel once more and makes for the door, the handle of which he grips like a shipwreck survivor plunging fingers into dry land. "I also leave up there the shame that none of you could understand or even feel, not even if you spent a hundred years trying." Alcántara Carnero unlocks the door, and hearing the click pulls on the handle with his huge hands. The chink of light becomes a rectangle as the door's four rusted hinges pose their rasping questions:

Really think you're leaving all that?

Truly believe your fury, anger, and shame will stay just where you left them?

That you have it in you to free yourself?

"I don't know, but I do know that I'm leaving," he says. Ourman steps into the rectangle of light, putting an end to the moment he has been waiting for so long, the moment that, for all that it should not have, begins our story.

CONCEPTION

IT IS ALSO A CROSS SECTION, this story, of the moments that shine beaconlike in the murk of Germán Alcántara Carnero's existence. Glittering instants that might've been placed at beginning, middle, or end—the cruxpoints in the life of ourman—these being a murder, the flight of two young men abroad, the unfolding of a war, the death of a child, one uprising, one love affair, one conflagration that consumed two dogs, the unveiling of one great dam—some bitterness, some condolences, many bullets, a religious conversion, much rage, and the conception of a being Félix Salvador Germán Alcántara Arreola and María del Pilar y del Consuelo Carnero Villalobos never imagined would be important enough to have his story remembered.

A story that might just as well have begun here: August 8, 1901, a moment in which the pigeons abruptly fall quiet, as though on some sudden command, and when Félix Salvador Germán Alcántara Arreola regains consciousness, having had a weeklong fever, and is instantly offended by the stench of his own body: oh sweet, oh acid fetor. *How long have I been lying here?* He does not know how long, and lets out a moan, more animal than human, while, at the far end of the shack we have just entered, María del Pilar y del Consuelo Carnero Villalobos parts the ragged, sun-blanched drape in the doorway and ducks outside.

Félix Salvador Germán Alcántara Arreola, third child of José Germán Froylán Argenis Alcántara Castillo and Hilda Heredí Arreola Avella, gradually comes to his senses. He keeps his eyes shut a little longer, and with the bitter taste of fever still on his lips, runs his hands along the cloth beneath him, damp from all the sweats. He feels the warmth of day on his skin, and hears the owl's *too-whoo* cut across by the cawing of a magpie shooed by his wife a moment ago. It is the hour when the sounds of the day mutate: croaking of frogs gives way to buzz of cicadas, donkeys' braying replaces cock-a-doodle-doos, and the constant chorus of dog barks gives way to the grief-stricken call of a coyote.

With much effort, Félix Salvador Germán Alcántara Arreola—whom we will also refer to as Félix Salvador— begins hefting himself onto his left side, and after a few moments' struggle succeeds, shifting onto one very ample hip and the leg that hurts him nowadays in cold weather. For four years now, such simple actions have been a trial.

María del Pilar y del Consuelo Carnero Villalobos, meanwhile, rolls up her sleeves as she moves across the yard, glancing at the sierra beyond, the vastness of this land. The sun is but a handspan from the tops of the mountains, and a faint shadowy haze has settled over the earth, itself pinpricked by hundreds of infinitesimal bright lights—fireflies whose tiny luminescences seem to María del Pilar's eye like so many floating splinters. Strange, but it is a shimmering spectacle that Félix Salvador Germán Alcántara Arreola has never contemplated, and in any case he, lying where he is currently lying, now has other things on his mind.

After pausing to catch breath, restoring his lungs to their usual labored rhythm, Félix Salvador tenses his jaw and, straining, kicking his legs like an upturned beetle, he finally succeeds in rolling onto his back. The pestilent little eddy of dust raised in this maneuver eventually drifts back down again, settling on the body, still quivering from effort, of this corpulent man.

In the last four years, Félix Salvador Germán Alcántara Arreola has put on ninety pounds, and more is yet to come: within seven years his weight will be double what it is now, and at that point he will no longer be able to get up. A red, swollen welt upon the ground, a pustule of anger and rage that will poison the lives of his daughters and his son. His entire lineage, and even the men and women who merely happen to live in his vicinity, will be affected by his malignance, a malignance I, too, am fighting—but we will come to that. For now, the only thing that matters is the woman filling a wash pail outside, spilling a little onto earth so dark it could be mistaken for ash: María del Pilar y del Consuelo Carnero Villalobos, who cups water out of the pail with her hand like a dog's tongue laps up water.

She fears dust more than anything, and she lives in a place where dust is all there is. Her wet footprints follow their mistress over to a pool in a rocky hollow. María del Pilar y del Consuelo Carnero Villalobos—whom we will

refer to as María del Pilar y del Consuelo or as simply
María del Pilar from now on—does not hear the church
bells ringing on the other side of the plain, in distant Lago
Seco, the town where our story began—a place where, I
insist, it should not have begun. Here, on this flank of the
Mesa Madre Buena, it should have begun here, where the
sound of the church bells from Lago Seco, accompanied
by the sound of two other bells now pealing across the
Mesa, combines to resemble that of glass buckling—
cracking but not quite shattering—more closely than it
does metal striking metal. The two bells that accompany
Lago Seco's principal bell are not nearby, either: one is in
the grounds of the mesa's main hacienda and the other
is in the tower of the church on the mountainside, hard
to access between sheer scarps and gullies.

Here, without leaving María del Pilar—remaining
at her side as she inexpressively scoops up water with
her pail—here now is the story of the church on the
mountainside: the story of February 17, 1934, a day when
Germán Alcántara Carnero, accompanied by Will D.
Glover and El Demónico Camilo Mónico Macías Osorio,
reduced the church to a rubble of charcoal and bent
nails. Teobaldo, the boss on the mesa at that time, who

had in years gone by provided work for half the people in these lands, the same lands in which this present chapter unfolds, twelve hours earlier had given the order: "Burn that church tomorrow, and no fucking up. I don't want a single one of those bastard priests left alive, and I don't want them scurrying their way past you, either. That's where they get together to plot and scheme. You, go hide out between the buildings, and I'll go do the same in the scrub up there. Some of you go into town, and the rest of you stake out that empty lot."

The empty lot being the place we left María del Pilar y del Consuelo, back in August 8, 1901, as she put down the pail and looked over at a spot a couple of meters away, at the ashy soil and at the worms that her trail of water had brought writhing to the surface. *Like smoke from a fire*, she thinks. Then, without knowing why, she says aloud: "Worms, but like smoke turning and twisting, writhing on the ground . . . "—to which I'll add: like the smoke that rose from the church that El Gringo Alcántara, El Demónico, and Will D. Glover burned down on February 17, 1934. They had set out six hours earlier, and it wasn't till the sun was up and they came in sight of the church—where the majority of the rebels had gone to sleep the previous night—that they posted their horses, unloaded the jerrycans and their weapons, and set forth on foot, no one saying a word, crawling for the last forty meters. Ahead of them, peace enveloped the church, chrysalislike.

By the time the doors of the church were being pushed on from the inside, Teobaldo and Will had already shut them from the outside. The dying men shrieked and battered on the door, but could not sway the men whose trio of chains kept it shut fast. The bells, normally silent at that hour, began to chime. The bell tower, which El Gringo Alcántara had scaled earlier with the help of an insider paid off by Teobaldo, had been doused with the contents of the jerrycans they'd dragged up the path. The black billowing thread of smoke reached skyward, a tongue mute and never-ending, twisting back and around on itself like María del Pilar's worms. By the time the two tall church windowpanes exploded, the ten men shut inside were also exploding: before the flames could reach them, the heat had boiled them alive.

Before leaving what was by now a heap of charcoal and bent nails, El Gringo Alcántara, taking in his arms a small Christ that had somehow escaped the flames, spotted a body in the distance: "There's someone behind those rocks!" he yelled. But now is not the moment to follow him as he gives chase; now we go back to María del Pilar—who was sent to the Mesa Madre Buena as a young girl in order to keep her from an epidemic that had struck several towns around her family's home, and who does not hear the bells in the distance—cannot hear the bells in the distance—being that she is deaf.

Inside the small shack, Félix Salvador does hear the bells and, still delighted at his success—at having managed to roll over—entertains the idea of this trio of bells chiming in celebration of his recovery. He is, he decides, not feeling feverish but just hot, nauseated, too, and, having once more emerged from a feverish affliction that troubles him from time to time—a result of the day when his system first shut down—thinks: *Just need to get this cover off.* Shuffling his feet back and forth, back and forth, he manages to do so—the sight is something like seeing an anaconda emerge from a chrysalis.

Only when Félix Salvador's body is revealed in its fullness, bathed in sweat and covered in welts, does the gravity of his illness become clear. As his feverish body comes in contact again with the air, Félix Salvador, the first person in our story's lineage who thrives on anger and rage, and whom we will also consequently call *the-firstone*, feels better for an instant, and wonders if the time is right for him to peel open his eyes. He hasn't wanted to do so yet, fearing he might still be delirious, might again be showered with the scythes and sickles and awful lacerating implements that have been raining down in his hallucinations. Thefirstone opens his eyes and gradually discerns a white ray of light, one might almost say grayish if rays of light could be grayish. The sun, slipping behind the mountains, is spreading its most leadlike tones over the world, a late light that filters in through the roof beams. María del Pilar, meanwhile, leaning against the wall of the coop, decides she should go back now, where one of her daughters, María del Sagrado Alcántara Carnero, is crying, though in fact her mother cannot hear.

María del Pilar retraces her steps across the dark, powdery soil, and walks silently across the yard and past the slumbering dogs. The boastful vultures turn lazy circles high above, and every now and then smaller birds flit past as though shot from a catapult. In the shrubland, where a large dam will one day be built, the shacks begin to light up one after another, shimmering like torches as the men and women who live inside them, 39 adults and 180 children—all the youths and young men and women have left—light their stoves, their tallow candles, and their small lamps. Slowly but irremediably, the shadows thicken around these shimmering torches, robbing everything of color, texture, and shape.

Moving aside the threadbare cloth in the doorway, María del Pilar enters the place that has been her home for seven years, and sees that her husband is awake. He has succeeded in shifting the blanket off his naked body and rolling over. María del Pilar averts her gaze. Her disgust for this man, whose churning folds of flesh are near-black in color, is such that she simply does not want to be here. Glancing at the useless cloth across the doorway—still rippling slightly—María del Pilar feels a strong urge to go away and never come back. "I should, that's exactly what I should do," says the woman quietly, looking away from her husband so as to avoid his instructions—instructions to do things she doesn't want to do. His waking strikes her like a body blow.

As though sensing her, thefirstone turns his head around to the left, and the portion of the shack he previously could not see invades his two corneas—the one out of which he can see and the other one, the dead one. They watch each other in the thickening dark. Their disabilities mean the picture they form of each other is forever incomplete, but also that neither could survive in this kingdom alone. But let's be clear: their impairments are not the reason they married; this union came out of another kind of necessity: a time of poverty when the only things in abundance were hunger, coldness, and enervation. María del Pilar finds a candle and lights it.

Félix Salvador's good eye comes to rest on the figure that resolves in the candlelight, and desire immediately rushes out of its nothingness and everythingness to take hold of him. Something important is about to take place in this story—a moment that, hinge-like, joins the life of Germán Alcántara Carnero and the lives of his parents.

So our tale might just as well have begun here: August 8, 1901: The firstone, having moments before emerged from his illness, with his one functioning eye fixed on his wife's outline in the faint yellow light, starts to stroke his balls and cock. A longing has sprung up like a soldier hurtling forward at the sound of enemy fire. María del Pilar y del Consuelo, holding the candle that illuminates this moment, looks down on the movements of her husband's hands and at the tremoring of his good eye, which quivers incessantly: watching it quiver is like watching a rotten egg joggle slightly inside a jar. *He should've gotten up today*, thinks the woman who now places the candle down on the table. *If he had he'd be tired by now, dead tired after having gone up to the hacienda*, she thinks, looking at the network of scars on the forehead, temple, and left eyelid of her husband, whose desire seethes, close to boiling point.

As María del Pilar sees his hand go up, her second daughter starts crying on the other side of the shack, finally awoken by the other girl's wail. María del Pilar, who gave birth to the youngest of the girls four months earlier, does not register María del Sagrado and Heredí de los Consuelos's cries. Her skin, which often senses surrounding sounds, has gone numb at the sight of her husband's hand lifting, ordering her to come closer. A small pearl of sweat rolls down the woman's forehead and trembling face as she approaches the sweating, pulsing body of her husband, who has just drawn back his foreskin: the tip gleams like his dead eye. With a swift gesture out of keeping with his hulking frame, thefirstone throws himself forward and snatches up his wife's wrist. María del Pilar lets herself be pulled toward him, while her daughters wail so loudly that the dogs, awake now, begin to circle the shack.

Thefirstone's jaw slackens at the sight of her lifting her skirt, but then his face turns taut again: a strange movement behind his wife catches his eye, and he thinks he sees, through a gap in the boards that make up the wall, the scythe of his delusions come tumbling from the sky once more. Shaking his head like a dog shaking the water from its back, thefirstone hears his wife's knees creak, and sees her face, dissolved in sweat. Outside their shack, meanwhile, a trio of black vultures is feasting—it was these carrion birds that thefirstone mistook for the bastard scythes of his fever. In a matter of minutes, the ravenous birds will have devoured the coyote they are currently vying for, a coyote that was killed three or four days ago by a hunter and his dogs, whose collective fury widowed the female coyote that was wailing earlier on, just as the two girls now wail inside the shack.

The dogs, unsettled by the crying girls, have begun to bark. Hearing the barking and pulling down his wife's underwear, thefirstone is taken back to a day, long ago, when he and his brothers looked up at the horizon and saw an enormous dust cloud approaching, drawing behind it a dry, intermittent, drumlike noise. A wall of dust coming at them. The cloud cleared a number of minutes later, revealing a hundred horses galloping forward, however many howling dogs there were, and a huge mass of men shouting and whistling. When this ocean reached them—stock still and enchanted by a strong and strange sensation he would later try to describe by saying: "It was both longing and fear, both at once"—thefirstone begged the riders to take him with them, riders accompanied by the same pack of dogs that went on to beget the hounds currently barking in the yard outside.

As happens whenever barking starts up among a pack of dogs and there is no reason for it, the barking soon turns to snarling, and the animals turns on one another. The smallest animals capitulate first, followed by the sickly and then the old, and the yard only falls quiet again once all the dogs bar two—the two strongest and most vicious—have been vanquished, a quiet broken by the wailing of the girls, by the panting, gasping, and huffing of thefirstone, and by the cries of María del Pilar y del Consuelo—whom we should not now refer to by her full name, but simply as "consuelo," which after all is the word for "solace." As this violence is inflicted on her, consuelo succeeds in imagining herself elsewhere. For the first time, she finds she truly hates this man with his arms around her; a hate that will only grow from this day forward. *Blind son of a bitch*, she says inside her head. Her husband has never told her the story of how he lost his eye, has not told her, that is, that he lost it in a skirmish with the police when his horse, startled by bullets and cannonballs flying, threw him onto some rocks, one of which, sharpened by wind and rains, was only too happy to relieve him of his sight.

How well my deafness has suited you, consuelo thinks, still staring into the dead eye. *How convenient, never having to explain yourself.* She is full of hate, it expands inside her and she opens her mouth while saying inwardly: *How convenient for you, to never have to hear me say a word*—and then spits into her husband's dead eye. Thefirstone feels the impact of it, wonders what it is, but before he has worked it out another gob of spittle has landed at the center of the doughy gray scar of his blindness. "What the fuck are you doing?" he says, not out loud but rather with a gesture of his hands and mouth, and the only reply he gets is to be spit on once again. Furious, thefirstone wraps his arms around the body on top of him, and, pushing down on the coarse cold thighs with which she is trying to lift herself off his lap, shoves himself into her. Chin on his wife's shoulder, Félix Salvador Germán Alcántara Arreola shuts his eyes as her warm saliva drips from his face in the same way blood dripped from it on the day of the accident: *If only it had been just my eye*, he thinks, even as he thrusts into her. *If only I hadn't ended up alone as well.* He shoves his wife's face back and, his frenzy increasing, bellows, "They left us to die. They told us to get out of there, and told us that what we thought wasn't enough, was actually got more than we deserved."

With a few cracks of his neck, thefirstone shakes away the memories that are close to submerging him completely, and raises his huge haunches from the earthen floor, lifting his wife up with him. As though trying to insert his entire body into her. For her part, she only wants this moment to end. "Go on, you animal, get it over with," this woman says to herself in silence, using other words, words from a language she made up long ago. "Get it over with, and let me go," she says. Félix Salvador opens his mouth and, throwing his head back, spews up a viscous sort of yowl, fingers juddering as a shock runs through him, an earthquake throughout his entire body. Spent, his seed deposited, he rolls back onto the ground and pushes the woman off him, dribble running down over his jowls and chest and a good part of his abdomen. He then very slowly begins coming back to himself and, on noticing his daughters crying, the youngest and the other one, the one born with a puckered face and a lolling tongue, points to the other side of the shack. You: go.

Consuelo lifts her face and, feeling the seed of hate gaining purchase deep in her body, gets up. One of the girls must be crying. As she crosses the space, the light from the candle sets her features trembling—features that have grown hard with rancor and that now fail to find the configuration previously known to them. She is changed, a woman whose every inch now complies with an order she utters in a language that is solely her own: "You: stop your trembling."

María del Pilar's dislocated expression will from this day on be her only expression and this her body with its hard new armature of courage or anger, anger she will pass on to sons and daughters alike. When she reaches the girls and finds them both crying, her anger evaporates and shame flushes through María del Pilar, every inch of her. She feels an urge to go to the well, to plunge naked into it, and to stay there feeding on mud forever.

The dogs outside, spent from their fight, descend into sleep, borne down by the low song of María del Pilar y del Consuelo, behind whom thefirstone falls asleep in an instant. His dreams are of the years before his illness, his years as an outlaw. As the candlelight trembles, its wick about to expire, the two girls, calm now, look up at the woman as she places them gently back down before opening her arms wide, bringing her legs together, opening them again when she feels how wet they are, arching her back, and getting up and going over to the doorway, passing through it and out into the night, the massive darkness that buries everything. This is the same darkness that ourman will look upon each sundown of the year between his decision to leave the ministry and the day that awaits us at the turning of this page, a day about which, if this story yet had no beginning, it might be possible to say: this is when it begins.

FORTUNA

JUNE 14, 1957: a day we arrive in having crossed the high mesa once more and a little over half a century, a day that holds within it a moment unusually bright in the life of Germán Alcántara Carnero. A moment that could be this story's beginning, were it not for the fact that this story has no beginning and, of course, for the fact that it is concerned only with the knots in a thread—and not with its ends or with its length. Our story is concerned only with the moments that hinder the unspooling of a life: four men torturing a priest; a young man crying out from inside a bolted iron trunk; two young people fleeing abroad; a young man confronting his father; men having ears and eyelids cut off; a brother asking: "Where is my sister?"; a woman who, having given birth moments earlier, hears someone say: "Sickly"; and a man, this man before us right now, in fact, who is currently, tentatively, knocking on the door of a home.

Puzzled that no one comes to the door, this man we are now seeing for the first and last time—thick spectacles, very thin mustache, long mane of hair—lifts his face and sees a flock of birds flying low to the ground. In the morning light their feathers are strangely silver, and the sky is a deep, metallic indigo. He scans the house of the woman he awaits, peers at roof, cornices, yellow walls, door—a woman whose life is going to touch that of Germán Alcántara Carnero's, who, a year after giving up his work, is still trying to ascertain what to want as much as what to do, all while trying to figure out what made him think this openness is what he wanted, what he was missing. "Still haven't figured it out?" thefirstone's son asks himself in the early hours every day. "What you must do to put an end to this sleeplessness, this restlessness, this searching? Did you not say you would put all the guilt behind you when you left, all the shame? Didn't you say that peace lay this way?" But though this is his story, Germán Alcántara Carnero, currently racking himself in the massive, silent darkness of Lago Seco, is not at this moment of any importance, unlike this other man now rapping on the door.

"I'm going to knock this door down if she doesn't get out here," he says to himself, a man of middling height whom we will very soon forget, in the same way that ourman goes on to forget about him. *What the hell is keeping her?* he asks himself, looking at his watch and eagerly, or rather anxiously, turning and pacing a little way to the left. Coming to the window, he gets up on tiptoes to look in, but the light on the glinting glass prevents him from getting a good look inside.

It is the time of day when people are out on the streets of Lago Seco, when children go to school and their parents go to work, the time of day when dogs scavenge piles of trash and cats slink back to their resting places. Worried about the time, this man, neither large nor small but whose clothes are too small for him and who wears children's shoes and a tie that could be a hangman's noose, goes back to the door and knocks once more—harder this time, the sound much like the one made by Germán Alcántara Carnero as he slams the door of his house behind him: he has been up late again and decides to take a walk to see if going out might help him fend off his past and maybe silence the voices he has been hearing since the day he quit: *weren't you going to become something else?* But now is not the time to speak of this.

Now is the time to orbit this man, a being so average, even his innermost yearnings are paragons of moderation—let us then call him *middling*. Having paced around a little more, leaned against a wooden post, looked at his watch, and walked a short distance from the house, middling marches up to the door and begins pounding on it. Inside, the three women sit bolt upright in the bed, extricate themselves from one another, and hurry to the door. The sound of their clattering footfall resounds in the hallway, where a figure of Christ is hung and where a dull white light bounces off of floor tiles that are the color of milk when it boils. Hearing the footfall, middling stops knocking, and the grandfather clock in the parlor strikes as the sisters bid their hurried farewells. One of them opens the door and the other two move aside. They cannot embrace as they would have hoped to, and their imagined, impossible embraces become lodged in their bodies, and there they will remain.

When the door swings open, middling takes a step forward and, pointing to his watch, cries out: "We're going to be late again! We're not going to make the appointment. I told you to be ready—I told you." "Oh," says this woman with a smile and a squint—5'2", brown-skinned, firm-fleshed, though by Lago Seco standards she is positively tall, lean, and alabaster-white—"I've left my papers. Won't be a second." And she dives back into her parents' home—the canaries and larks in the inner courtyard cease their singing when she comes through— and dashes into her father's study, hunting through the writing desk, grabbing a bundle of papers, and going back out to the street, where middling points to the hands of the watch that so concern him. "It's after eight already. Just let me know when you intend for us to leave. Maybe they'll just wait another six months, or another year." Her smile turns to laughter as she pulls shut the door of her home, where Germán Alcántara Carnero is very soon to make an appearance. Turning the key in the lock, she takes middling's arm, which he sulkily proffers.

The sun rises calmly into the sky, its metallic and now orange-tinged rays lighting up the birds, the edges of a cloud that is gradually drifting farther away, the cats posted around on the enclosing walls of homes, the bark on the wooden stakes, the highest leaves on the trees, and the tops of the palm trees ourman ordered be planted all across the Mesa Madre Buena. As they turn at the corner of Candelaria and Nombre del Señor, middling, still angry, shakes off the woman's arm and says: "You were supposed to be ready when I came—*before* I came!" And again she laughs and makes no reply. "Come on," he says, "there's still a way to go yet."

The streets they are still to reach are the same ones that separate Germán Alcántara Carnero from the town square, and if we look up at the sidewalk ahead, we'll see him there, dragging his feet, arms hanging like heavy vines, immersed in thought: *How to make this pain go? How to make myself forget?* And, as on the last three hundred and however many mornings, his answer is the same: *Not by going back to the ministry. I need to find whatever it was that made me give it all up to begin with!*

A car passes on the street, the sound of its motor catching the couple's attention but not that of ourman. We will eventually come back to middling and the woman, who has quickened her pace somewhat, so that she is now advancing as briskly as ourman, for all that ourman has no particular destination, and only wants to tire himself out, only wants to find a way to sleep.

A second car comes along the street, its tailpipe spluttering and making Germán Alcántara Carnero jump—thinking he's heard a gunshot—*Maybe you miss all that?* he asks himself, alarmed. *Maybe that's what you're yearning for? But how could you be, if that's all you think about, if the very second I even think about laying my head on a pillow, I see her bleeding again, her dying white hands, her eyes going dim, that helpless look!* Immersed as he is, Germán Alcántara Carnero walks straight out onto Unión de San Antonio, where a car nearly hits him. The driver starts insulting him, but then, seeing who it is, immediately stops and speeds off.

Startled more by his dragging tiredness than by the accident he has just narrowly avoided, Germán Alcántara Carnero quickens his pace. *Must find what it is that you don't have. Stop thinking about what you had before. God knows what it is, but you can still try to look, who knows, you might chance upon it.* In fact, his quest is nearly at an end. Coming to the town square, he stops, recalling the day he laid these flagstones and thus temporarily letting go of his inner questioning, this inner siege. His eyes reflect the people crossing the space, the motionless trees at even intervals, the glistening water in the fountains, the glass plates in the streetlamps, and the worn-down metal benches.

Do you truly not see it? That you just need to admit you were wrong? Germán Alcántara Carnero asks himself, stumbling once more into his memories and raising his enormous hands to protect himself from the sparks flying off the blacksmith's stall ahead. *To just accept that you were wrong to think you could simply walk away?* Repeating these questions, he sets off with the quick skip of a startled horse. A couple of meters away, meanwhile, the man we have already begun to forget is shouting at his woman: "Come on, hurry it up—we might still make it! It'll be tight, but we might!" "I can't run anymore," says the woman who has now crossed the same number of streets as ourman and has arrived in the square at the same time as him. "If you'd bothered to be on time, we wouldn't have to run!" says middling, turning to the person he is dragging along, who, stopping, says: "We wouldn't even be here, you mean, if you weren't as stubborn as a mule," at which she pulls up and ourman, coming the opposite way, crashes into her. Down she goes, crashing into middling in the same way that this moment crashes into our story, a story in which, at

08:17 on June 14, 1957, three lives become entangled and simultaneously derailed.

This trio, now piled together on the ground, stare at one another wordlessly. Had middling seen ourman coming he would have done everything he could to avoid him, for all that it would have made the couple later still. Disentangling their limbs but not their lives, these beings we have been watching look away from one another and, still not saying a word, begin examining themselves: knees, palms of hands, wrists, elbows, and shoulders. People in the square veer past them, the cooing of the unsettled doves in the trees drifts down, while in the distance, a buzz or murmur grows: a flock of sparrows comes into view, their little gray bodies dropping on the square like a downpour. While ourman makes to get up, the cooing doves begin to lift their heavy selves skyward.

What on earth am I thinking, Germán Alcántara Carnero asks himself, *walking around without looking where I'm going?* Propping himself up on one arm, he continues: *Actually, what were these two idiots thinking?* He brings his other arm around onto the flagstones and turns to look at the person lifting up his torso and head. Before he's had a chance to tell middling what he thinks of him, there is a noise like an explosion on one corner of the square: a truck has stopped on Calle Sufragio Efectivo and in its bed, attached to a steel bar, stands a huge pink pig, so large it could almost be a flayed cow. Gouts of smoke are coming from the truck and continue to do so even when the owner of vehicle pops the hood and unscrews the cap that was smothering the engine. *He shouldn't have taken it off quickly like that when it's hot*, thinks ourman, eyes trained on the truck. *Why did we have to crash into someone now, and why did it have to be into this man?* the man we have nearly forgotten asks himself, not daring to grumble or even ask after his woman's injuries.

Eventually, Germán Alcántara Carnero cries out: "What the hell were you thinking, not looking where you're going?" Straightening up, bringing his weight to bear on his two knees and on the tips of his shoddy old shoes, rolling his head forward, back, and then to both sides, Alcántara Carnero realizes the blow his shoulder just sustained has awakened a wound that hasn't bothered him for a number of years: an impact that shattered his shoulder and split it in three one morning long ago—a morning whose details are not however required in the telling of this story. Now our story dissects this moment, a moment in which ourman demands to know, as he puts his hand to his shoulder: "Are you fucking blind?" And it is the woman who answers: "You've got eyes in your head, too. Why didn't you see us?" And, laying her hands across her breast, the place where the shoulder of this individual struck her, the woman we are watching says once more, as middling looks on in terror, "You were coming straight at us, too. You could have looked."

The doves that flew up above the square a moment ago turn in the air one last time before coming to rest on the roofs, the cornices, the drainpipes, and the walls of the homes and buildings of Lago Seco, a city that for fifteen years—since the government gave the order that everyone become a pig farmer—has given off a stench of guts, blood, pigskin, and pigsties. Alcántara Carnero lets out a laugh, astonished to hear anyone speak to him like this, and, taking his hand down from his shoulder, turns to look to his left. "Is it me you're talking to like that?" he asks the woman, her head still bowed so that all he can see is the cascade of her hair. "I said, is it *me* you're talking to like that?" Looking up, she says: "Who else? Can't you tell this one doesn't say much?" and she points at middling, who has a hard rock of fear inside him, one that keeps him pinned to the ground: "Shut up, woman!" he shouts. "It's our fault. We were arguing, *we* didn't look." "I don't need you to make excuses for me!" cries the woman, exasperated. She pierces Alcántara Carnero with a look, and his rage sinks into her black eyes—like a red-hot tool sinking into a bucket of dark, icy water. *Do you remember now, all those things you said you'd do once you left, all those things you said you'd leave behind?* Alcántara Carnero asks himself, unable to take his eyes from her jet-black pupils. For a minute, which feels like a second to ourman and like a lifetime to middling, the woman's gaze and that of Germán Alcántara Carnero become entwined, he murmuring all the while: "So this is it . . . what I needed . . . what I should have done . . . this is what was missing," and then, louder, words he has not spoken in many a year: "Are you all right?" "It hurts here," says the woman, pointing to her chest, then the knee and ankle of one leg, "and here and here." Growing calmer, she turns to middling, who, sensing what is happening, overcomes his fear and finally picks himself up.

So this was what I should have been trying to find . . . and this is how it ends!—while aloud: "Where does it hurt? What can I do? Can I get you anything?" The truck on the corner starts up again and the sparrows make as though to fly away, an upwards feint, but settle straight back down on their branches. "We're fine," answers middling. "We don't need your help," he says, replying to a question that wasn't meant for him and placing himself between ourman—who feels his ribs lurching in a sudden and unfamiliar way—and the woman—whose knee hurts. Examining it, she says: "What do you know about what I need or don't need? Since when have you been a doctor or a nurse?" At the sound of her voice, Alcántara Carnero feels that strange lurch in his chest once more. Plunging himself once more into her eyes of ash, ourman takes a step, shoves the other man away, and—all the while thinking: *the only way I'll become someone else is by making a family*—offers her his hand. "Let me help you, I can take you to the Otero Hospital. That leg's really bleeding, and it was my fault." A few meters away, next to the smallest fountain in the square, a pair of pigeons that have been fighting over a female bird fall to the ground. Their squawking startles middling, but not ourman or the woman, who continue to look straight at each other. "Let me h-help you," says Alcántara Carnero, surprised. Never before have his words come stumbling out like this.

Middling, heart close to exploding and hands like ice—petrified because he recognized ourman the moment he saw him—stands between him and his partner: "No, no, it was our fault. Please, we're okay." But ourman ignores this, holding out both hands in the shadow of the fountain, where a third male pigeon comes fluttering down—an opportunist moving in as the other pigeons begin to flag—and brushes his fingers against the woman's skin, drawing a laugh and a reply from her: "The Otero Hospital won't be open at this hour." Middling, desperate now, says: "They won't see us if we're late. Here, let me help you up . . . They might, just might still let us in." "Might let us in," sneers the woman, as middling, poor middling, tries to make a show of bravery even in the face of an overwhelming terror, and again says: "Come on. There's no time to mess around now. Really, truly, we have to hurry. We still might talk them round." Taking ourman's left hand and middling's right hand, the woman finally allows herself to be lifted to her feet, only, once she is up, to break down laughing. Neither of the men understand this, but nor do either them let go of her strong, slender fingers.

Middling, ignoring his woman's ongoing laughter as well as the memory called to mind by the presence of

ourman—a memory of pain, humiliation, and abuse—
with an unexpected rush of anger, punches away the wrist
of Germán Alcántara Carnero. "Let go of her hand! She
is a lady! No one here wants anything from you!" The
woman, astonished, turns to him. "What is with you?
It's hardly . . . he was just trying to help." Why middling
might have reacted like this, she can't imagine—unaware
as she is that it has nothing to do with being late, nor
with jealousy, unaware as she also is that these two men
have met before, on a day I will now speak of though only
very briefly, since, after all, this story does not belong to
middling—a man who, along with a dozen other men,
was part of a public protest on the main drag of Lago Seco
on October 28, 1949, three days before All Saints' Day.
Middling and a number of other farmers, having come
under the sway of a demented priest, demanded that the
slaughterhouses change their methods and stop killing
pigs in such cruel ways. They could no longer stand aside,
they said, while the animals suffered so unnecessarily.
It had fallen to Germán Alcántara Carnero to clear the
protesters, and he took most of his men down in the late
afternoon—the time of day when gnats come out in force.
The police, following his orders, surrounded the precinct

and waited for nightfall before cutting off the electricity supply. Once the area had been plunged into darkness, ourman and his men burst in, firing their guns into the air, and began shouting and beating the twelve men, who lay on the ground hugging themselves and trembling in fear. They dragged the twelve farmers over to a blood-stained yard used for washing pigskins and tied them up while ourman taunted them: "*Really* want to stop seeing those piggies suffer, don't you? *Really* want to stop hearing their little squeals, huh?" Then, to his men: "So cut off their eyelids and their ears." As I have said, though, this took place a long time ago and on a day that sheds no light on the life of Germán Alcántara Carnero, which is also why he does not remember this other man whose hair falls over the scars where his ears once were and the rims of whose glasses obscure the marks around his eyes. This is not this maimed man's story, and we would do well to return now to June 14, 1957, the day ourman met the woman who would later become his wife.

"Seriously, what is it?" says the woman, pointing at middling's flushed skin. "Look at you, you look like you're about to combust"—this draws a laugh from ourman, who cannot and does not want to look away from the obsidian eyes that glimmer whenever the woman laughs—a laughter middling cannot stand—it burns in his eyes and in his ears like alcohol burns in a wound—and now he drops the hand he grasped less than half an hour ago outside the woman's front door. Taking no notice, she says to ourman: "Really think the hospital will be open?" They form a knot, this trio, and one strand now loosens and slips free, allowing the other two to clinch together more tightly. Middling, nearly forgotten now, turns and begins walking away. No longer average-sized but small, so small he's practically nonexistent, middling swallows his pride and keeps walking, heading toward the opposite end of the square, where a squirrel and two pigeons are squabbling over a piece of dry bread. He sidesteps some sparrows, none of which move out of the way for him, and threads his way through the people and the street dogs slumbering on the ground.

Ourman and the woman whose name he has just asked both turn toward the street, where a man is riding by on a bicycle, and she says, "Dolores Enriqueta," looking down as she walks, then looking off into the distance, then at her hands, then at the ground again, and then again at her hands. The sun's orange hue has now altered to a pale yellow, prompting Dolores Enriqueta to think: *Perhaps I am ill.* "And what is your surname?" asks El Gringo, surprised by how quickly his questions come. "Celis Gómez; Dolores Enriqueta Celis Gómez." A few meters from these two—neither of whom can imagine the deep unhappiness that awaits them as a couple—the pigeon that managed to beat its two tired foes in corralling the female coos in victory. No longer aware of the people passing silently on either side or of the heat or of the light glinting off everything, the couple we are following, whom we will call from this moment on *ourcouple*, comes to the corner of Sufragio Efectivo and Candelaria. "And where is your home?" Germán Alcántara Carnero then asks Dolores Enriqueta Celis Gómez, who gestures toward the end of the street and says: "71, Nombre del Señor."

Ourcouple turn and look into each other's eyes again, this time smiling. Something tells her that she has found a good man, and him that he has found the mother of his future children. Neither Germán Alcántara Carnero nor Dolores Enriqueta Celis Gómez can imagine the tragedy that will eventually engulf the birth of their first child, or the misfortunes that will befall their two other two children—a blow so great that it will engulf Dolores

Enriqueta in the same sadness she will experience upon the birth of her first child, the child to whom Germán Alcántara Carnero will dedicate himself body and soul until the day comes when he will dedicate himself body and soul to a faith he had formerly, for nearly six decades, repudiated and set himself against. But many years have yet to pass before then, and this current moment is still not at an end.

Germán Alcántara Carnero and Dolores Enriqueta Celis Gómez stroll in silence, as though for the thousandth time, making their way along the streets that lie between the town square and the home we visited briefly when this moment first began to unfold, a home I later resided at for a number of years and which this woman, four months from now, will depart for good.

But at this point in the story—a story that finally knows where its beginnings might have been and that knows, too, that I myself will be a knot in its thread—the only thing of import is to turn to the moment that shines least light on the life of our man—a moment that, were someone else to tell this story, might be placed at the beginning, but to organize the life of Germán Alcántara Carnero thus—for it is a life that has no beginning—would be sorely ill suited.

BIRTH, ILLUMINATION

NOW FOR THE MOMENT that sheds the least light on the life of ourman—a moment we arrive in having crossed the mesa and a span of fifty-five years, two months, and eight and a half days—a moment that, as I said before, would be our beginning if this story weren't being told by me, or indeed if there were no knot in its thread linking my life to the life of ourman. We will come to this knot in time, but for now, what matters is this moment: María del Pilar y del Consuelo Carnero Villalobos, as the sun beyond the laden fig tree struggles to break through the wooden slats of the old chicken coop, feels a jabbing in her innards and, rolling down her skirts, observes movement at the surface of her belly. She is a number of weeks short of term, yet here are the pains she has only known previously in labor: a fire kindled inside her abdomen, her breasts, and her belly button; and her vagina suddenly like a teeming anthill.

Tearing her eyes as best as she can from that frenzied sensation between her legs, and wresting her patience from the moment she finds herself in—a moment that, as I have already said, sheds little light on the life of ourman and that a different narrator might have used to open the faucet of this tale—María del Pilar y del Consuelo Carnero Villalobos lifts her hand and vigorously waves it through the air, swatting at the tiny white flies that for a number of minutes have been showing an interest in the sweat beading around her pores. This huge brigade rises to the ceiling, where a trio of beetles are sharpening their copper-colored wings and a shadowy moth wakes and begins flying against a beam until, insensate, it drops onto this woman's contracting belly—at which she, making a pincer of her fingers, grabs it and squeezes until it bursts: her fingertips shimmer with the pale and pearly dust of the dead insect in the same way this moment shimmers in the life of ourman—a moment that rather than lighting up the whole length of a life, sheds light on its fugitive breadth.

María del Pilar y del Consuelo Carnero Villalobos rolls the squashed bug between forefinger and thumb and flings it through one of the cracks in the wall, where a magpie, raising its beak, swallows the insect and lets out a satisfied caw, which sets off the chorus of sounds that signifies the end of every afternoon in this place: frogs and toads, a donkey braying somewhere in the distance, an owl call cutting through the emptiness, and the rasping of cicadas that drifts up like murmured prayers drift up from the temple that ourman will one day raze, condemning it for good; another thing we will come to in time. Now though, deaf as she is, María del Pilar y del Consuelo Carnero Villalobos has no sense of the noises freighting the air outside, but she does know from the waning light in the coop that night is closing in. The sky outside is now an ancient gray mantle, the pasturelands growing turquoise blue, and the glowering, metallic scree field is suddenly a deep black pit. *I need to be quick about this, get this baby out of me and get out of here*, thinks this woman as jab after jab strikes at her innards, increasing in intensity all the time. "Quick, quick," she says to herself in her own inner language, one she made up many years ago.

Urged on by the fading light, by the sounds she does not hear but can nonetheless sense, and by the violence of the jabs ramming her insides harder and harder, María del Pilar y del Consuelo Carnero Villalobos grits her teeth, leans her weight onto the pile of corn she has been husking, shifts her feet in the black soil beneath her, and, moments before giving birth, arraigns herself: *My bones were aching early this morning, my feet have been swollen for days, I should not have let it come to this.* Digging her toes into the earthen floor, she takes a deep lungful of air, stretches her neck, tenses her back, and, eyes squeezed shut, tries to get up by pushing down on the corn—but cannot. But since the day of Germán Alcántara Carnero's inception she has felt hard and immovable in the face of any setback, and she takes another breath and repeats to herself: "Have to, have to, have to . . ." She tries to get up once more, but midway through this attempt a jab lacerates her whole body, an electric shock that expands as dampness expands inside a wall, sapping her strength so that she tumbles onto this dark soil that looks so much like ash.

Forcing her midriff forward and crying out, María del Pilar y del Consuelo sees shadows growing and airborne

insects moving: huge green beetles and grain moths and
flies and gnats, a pair of cicadas and a fantastic dung
beetle whose mercury wings gather the reflections of this
dying day—a day as dim as this moment, which has not
been called upon to illuminate the length of our thread,
but rather to show us the place where our thread joins
its bobbin—that is, where the life of a mother and her
son are fastened together. María del Pilar y del Consuelo
Carnero Villalobos stretches her arms and tenses her back
as hard as she can, and succeeds in grabbing onto the low
beam that crosses the coop: *Now*, she thinks. *Do it now*,
even as the thought crosses her mind that she will have
to clean up after herself, not wanting any of the intimate
results of her childbirth to be found by her husband—
who is yet to come back from work at the hacienda on the
far side of this plain, part of a land forgotten by god long
ago and known by its landowners as "our lands" instead of
by its name: the Mesa Madre Buena. Gripping the beam,
she tries to straighten up but a contraction shoots along
her bones and through her veins. This woman, whom
we will call for now *womanwhoholds*, cries out—almost a
howl—while one of the dogs in the yard pricks its ears
and lifts its muzzle off the ground, sniffing the air: dry

grass and roots; the smell of small birds and of seeds; beyond that, the smell of stones; of brackish water and of rusted metal; and even farther off, a feline smell: the small mountain lions of this region; and of coyotes.

Relieved to find that everything is in its proper place, resting snout on paws, it begins probing the smells of the silhouettes it can tell apart from the evening darkness—a darkness that has rendered María del Pilar y del Consuelo Carnero Villalobos blind as she sits back down, sweating into the earthen floor. While we were outside this woman tried again and again to lift herself up using the beam. *It's like it's turned to lead*, womanwhoholds thinks, looking down at her belly. Bringing a hand up to eye level and moving it away, only now does María del Pilar y del Consuelo realize how dark it has become, and finds herself traveling through time, with no intention to do so. She is suddenly in that long-ago night when her parents made her leave their home on the coast and come to this plain, thereby saving her from the epidemic that would soon claim them and her siblings when it rampaged along the Pacific coast and through the sierra inland. *How long until you come and join me?* María del Pilar remembers asking that night. In response, her father lifted a number of fingers on one hand—she could not make out the number in the darkness.

María del Pilar y del Consuelo, ridding herself of these inner shadows with a shake of her head, says to herself, "Maybe if I do it all at once, pull with my arms and push with my legs, maybe I can make it to the hut that way, use a bit of ash to wipe myself with, find some clean rags." Jaw clenched—as I have already said, this woman made the decision, a little over half a year before, never to give in to anything again—María del Pilar y del Consuelo, placing supporting hands beneath her belly and wheezing, becomes mired again in the shadows that are her own shadows. She sees her parents again and, perhaps realizing that this moment is not just any moment, she wonders why she never heard from them again, though she'd never known much about them anyway, only this: her father was born on this mesa but fled to the coast at a very young age and entered the army only to become a deserter later on. Her mother was a native of these lands, orphaned young and taken in by a Chinese family that had come to work the railroads, whose language she never learned, not a single word. Before María del Pilar y del Consuelo can shake the memory from her head once more, a further cramp or shock or spasm rocks her.

Curled up on the floor, womanwhoholds vomits up the harsh and rasping sound of the pain that is wracking her: a cry so curdling and cold it disturbs the world. "Have to get this baby out," María del Pilar y del Consuelo says to herself: "I can't stay here," lifting her head from the patch of mingled sweat and earth, getting her hands onto the corn again, lifting herself onto the chair, and looking over at the door, in which a shadow abruptly appears. The dog has come in, and is agitated at the sight of the woman, having never seen her overcome like this: her arms limp, hair dripping wet, breathing both deep and shallow, and a very strange scent about her.

Like a drowning man who sees he is not going to be saved, womanwhoholds fastens her hands onto the beam, tenses her back, and pushes down through her legs—one second, two, three, four seconds—until finally she has succeeded in straightening her legs. In the doorway, the dog sniffs the ground nervously and watches as its mistress straightens her back and, eyes on her feet, lets go of the beam. Her eyes have adjusted to the darkness and she can discern the scabs on her hands that could easily

be moles, and on the beam—as well as on the ground
and the walls and even the roof of this coop—a covering of broken eggshells, dry animal shit, bird feathers,
and bloodstains, all of it evidence of a cruel slaughter.
Sickness emerged victorious from this battlefield—a
sickness known among the men and women of the plain
as swollen kidney and defined by the experts in the following way: *Worse even than diarrhea, or the endolimax
nana parasite, bird flu, or the diseases known as "bluecomb"
and "blackbreast," the "swollen kidney" sickness submits the
animal to horrific bouts of pain and condemns it to die a
very slow death. Known also as "Marek's Disease," this illness
sends the infected animal's temperature soaring, weakens its
digestive system, and produces a thick, foul-smelling diarrhea.
The vital organs eventually become inflamed and the nervous
system shuts down. The final state of this illness is character-
ized by the innards of the bird rotting, forcing it to expel, via
its anus and beak, a violet-colored mucus that contains its
own liquefied organs, a mucus that furthermore will infect
the ground of the pen or coop irrevocably.* (Perhaps this is
why only pigs, and the occasional cow, are now raised
on this mesa.) *In its earliest stages, however, the only effect
of Marek's Disease, named after Julius Marek, is to numb the*

legs of the infected bird. Once it is infected, its legs will give way constantly, just like the legs failing to support María del Pilar y del Consuelo Carnero Villalobos, whose knees wobble, ankles shake, and hips sway like a ship lists and sways in a storm. A couple of seconds later, womanwhoholds collapses, and as she lies on the ground some of the small white flies come to rest on her belly—a belly that, seen thus, in darkness and beneath her clothes, resembles more closely the swollen belly of a drowned person than that of a woman entering labor.

The dog grows increasingly unsettled, its sense of smell awash with the odors of this coop and with the smell now being exuded by María del Pilar y del Consuelo Carnero Villalobos. Instinct tells it to place a paw tentatively forward, keeping its eyes on the heap that is womanwhoholds, who feels the life inside her begin to writhe more violently still, the rage in its movements tearing at the membranes that separate her insides from the outside world—and her legs part. All at once, a draft of wind sweeps through the coop, and the dog and the woman turn their heads. The night has brought with it the gusts of sickness that blow across this mesa every six or seven months—winds that stop most plants from growing and that some people say come from the mines beyond the ridge of the mountains, and that others say originate in those places along the coast where animals are slaughtered. Here in this place where a great dam will one day be built, a dam that I have said we will visit when the time comes, winds stunt the growth of anything that is not an agave plant, a certain clumpy grass local to this area, mesquite trees, certain cacti, the odd thistle, the small, spiky *bisnaga*, the enterolobium pods, pepper trees, or the occasional fig tree.

The sulfurous dust and the infected wood chippings borne by these winds of sickness arrive in the coop accompanied by the sound of a bird flapping its wings somewhere in the distance, the smell of a decaying rabbit carcass somewhere else, and the sound of a rattlesnake nearby. María del Pilar y del Consuelo, though, does not pick up on the stink carried in by this wind—a smell so putrid that it forces the other dogs to their feet—and neither is she aware, of course, of the sounds accompanying the wind. She can contemplate nothing but what is going on in her innards, this struggle between her body and this other, smaller, seemingly molten body. Spreading her legs as wide as she can and resting her elbows on the floor, womanwhoholds lays her head back against the ground, raises her legs, and hooks her ankles over the beam she used a few moments ago to lift herself up. Above her body, in the space intersected by her moans and exclamations, the insects and bugs begin to swarm, frenzied: cicadas striking the roof in search of an opening, flies going up in eddies again, a scorpion raising its tail as the shimmering dung beetle approaches, and the spiders, feeling hopeful, poised at the edges of their webs.

Outside, meanwhile, the dogs that have been roused by the wind hurry near, approaching the place where the scent of their alpha mingles with that of María del Pilar y del Consuelo and with that of a creature who is new to their senses—a being who has decided the time has come to cut through the last two layers of the warm membranes that have until now held him inside his mother's womb. Her face changes—tenses with alarm—and she turns pale and trembles and her face seems to dissolve again and again. As her son presents his downy head to the world, womanwhoholds, little aware of why or of how she's doing so, contracts her muscles, squeezes her hips, flexes the tendons in her legs, and in the language she invented so many years ago, says: "I won't let you out . . .

I'm keeping you in me forever . . . I won't let him hurt
you, too." It has just struck María del Pilar y del Consuelo
Carnero Villalobos that her son—she somehow knows it
is a boy—will also be her husband's son, and this simple
fact is terrifying to her. It is curious that it should be here,
in the place where ourman will one day seek to alter the
unalterable, that María del Pilar y del Consuelo Carnero
Villalobos is now also attempting to alter the unalterable.

But before going on with the moment in which we
find ourselves, let us pause—a pause that will serve as a
window through which we can glimpse certain aspects
of other moments in time, for example the moment I
have just alluded to, which at the end of our story will
be further dissected:

January 4, 1950, the sun three-quarters into the course
that organizes a day, as Germán Alcántara Carnero gazes
into Anne Lucretius Ford's eyes and plunges his enormous hands into her blood-soaked midriff in an attempt
to keep Anne's blood from spilling from her. An hour
and a half earlier, and while they were crossing the vast
stretch of thicketland where, in the moment we have just
left and to which we will very soon return, ourman is
being born, Germán Alcántara Carnero and his partner

were ambushed by Ignacio del Sagrado Sandoval-Íñiguez Martínez and four of his men, who had followed them across the thicket, the rocky outcrop, and much of the scrubland where, with the bullets flying closer and closer, ourman said to his woman, pointing to a group of boulders: "Go in there. I'll be right behind you."

Perched at the top of a pepper tree that he quickly shinned up, Germán Alcántara Carnero waited for Ignacio del Sagrado and his men to come within range, and when they were finally close enough, he shot and injured three of them. When he went to take down the fourth—he was saving Ignacio del Sagrado for last—his gun, which had never failed him before in his life, jammed—and then the bullets began flying in one direction only. Letting himself drop like ripe fruit falling from a tree, Germán Alcántara Carnero abandoned the pepper tree and, as soon as he felt his legs make contact with the ground—the same ground upon which María del Pilar y del Consuelo Carnero Villalobos had once fought to keep her child inside her belly—began running toward the boulders where he'd left Anne Lucretius: a woman who'd come to this country so as to never be apart from ourman, a man who, we will see when the time comes, had to flee this country only later to flee the country he'd fled to. When Germán Alcántara Carnero finally reaches her, she is down on her knees, face streaming and a pool of blood forming on the ground beneath her.

Ourman lifts Anne Lucretius onto her feet and asks if she's able to run, and it takes all she's got—more than she's got—to even try; she cannot move at any kind of speed. Ignacio del Sagrado and his man are closing in, the bullets landing nearer and nearer. It is then that, as I said in the first chapter of our story and as I said at the beginning of this moment we are now observing, Germán Alcántara Carnero jumps down into a ditch, bringing Anne Lucretius in after him. Holding her in his arms, looking into her eyes, and placing his huge hands on the innards spilling from her, he asks: "Can you go on or not?" Shutting her eyes, she says, "I don't think I can take another step." Plunging his enormous forefinger two knuckles deep into the wound, so that her eyes shoot open, ourman repeats his question, though the reply is the same. Pushing his finger still farther in, Germán Alcántara Carnero moves right up close to the ashen face now two centimeters from his, begging once more: "Just one step . . . Or I could put you over my shoulders at least."

"Tell them I don't owe them anything. Tell them I don't know anything about this," Anne Lucretius says, or rather murmurs, in a tiny voice. Then, "You should get out of here before they come. Before those men get here." As she looks up at the sky, fixing her sight on the dimming gray mantle, ourman once more forces his finger into the burning wound through which her life is emptying, so that she will at least hear when he says, "Really think I'd leave you now?" To which, with a final smile, Anne Lucretius responds, "At least . . . at least you brought me here. At least I die having seen the place you were born." This was the reason they first came here together: she found it impossible to imagine his past. "Go, go," she says. "They must be nearly on us, even I can tell that," she insists, and with that her trembling legs give way, like the legs of a bird with Marek's Disease. Pushing his finger still farther in, ourman kisses Anne . . . but what he did next we do not see, because our view of it fades in the second Germán Alcántara Carnero removes his finger from the wound—gives up on trying to stop time and destiny—the same defiance shown by womanwhoholds as she attempts to stave off her son's birth, tries to draw the fragile body of ourman back inside her, concentrating

all her energy on her lower regions as another centimeter
of skull emerges from her, bloody and covered in black
hairs—short, stubbly black hairs like ants. Forcing her
shoulders down against the ground, María del Pilar y del
Consuelo arches her back and lets out a guttering howl,
further distressing the dogs gathered around the coop. A
flick of the tail and a quick flash of teeth from the alpha,
however, is enough to keep them at bay—only he gets to
be inside the coop, where womanwhoholds, though she
feels the whole head emerging, continues to try to suck
in and up and back. Such is the effort that an unnatural
fatigue immediately grips her, plunging her into a dark,
dense lethargy, while the rest of the body of ourman slips
toward life as a fish slips through clumsy fingers.

A second before tumbling into the chasm of uncon-
sciousness, she manages to take her child in her arms and
lie back down on the floor. Ourman immediately begins
to wail. Several minutes will pass before María del Pilar y
del Consuelo will regain consciousness, get up and leave
the coop, taking the newborn to the shack, into which
we will not follow them. Our story, a story that has now
illuminated the bobbin to which its thread is attached,
must now leave this hour, this day, this year. As María

del Pilar exits the coop, the alpha dog comes sniffing forward, then licks and chews and eventually gulps down the abandoned placenta—as rich and sweet to it as the mother's breast is rich and sweet to the child just born.

Stifling her child's cries with her body as she crosses the yard, María del Pilar y del Consuelo slips into the shack in which little María del Sagrado and Heredí de los Consuelos Alcántara Carnero are sleeping bundled together. Having lit the tallow candles and the stove, she gives ourman a wash and begins feeding him, taking in the sight of him, tenderly stroking him. Then, moving him from one breast to the other and looking up, she sees in the distance, framed by the doorway, a light coming across the scrubland: it is Félix Salvador Germán Alcántara Arreola returning from work, lamp in one hand, scythe in the other, soon to clear the dogs from his path, cross the yard, push aside the cloth over the doorway, and, in the instant we depart, find a scene that was not the one he had been expecting.

DECEPTION, REPARATION

FROM NOW ON, this story will dissect only the moments that illuminate a life in the same way that a lighthouse's twin beams illuminate the darkness: though lighting up two specific points, they also cast light on the darkness between them, just as knots in a thread give tension beyond just the fastened point: a young man fleeing and joining a band of fugitives, a giant dam, an uprising, a journey to another country, guilt, the longing with which one remembers the dead, the sadness of losing a woman and the joy of finding another one, violent parents and brutal children, the renunciation of certain principles, the desire to make an heir and the abjuration of what is seen in his eyes, the murder of a treacherous priest, and the moment when another priest—a priest who suddenly now comes into view—says at the top of his voice, shouting, possibly even reveling in it: "Sickly! The baby has been born sickly!"

What does that mean, "sickly"? Germán Alcántara Carnero thinks, jumping out of his chair and going over to the wooden door that separates the hallway in which we find ourselves and his room. "What does that mean?" he insists, while complaining inwardly: *I should have resisted her wishes. He should never have come into the house.* Ourman pelts the wood with his two enormous hands, but nobody answers. At the priest's announcement, the enormous room on the top floor of this house falls silent—a house built a number of years ago in lands that were worked by thefirstone and later by ourman. Germán Alcántara Carnero feels frightened—the cries of Dolores Enriqueta Celis Gómez have stopped, as have the sharp commands of the woman assisting her—and he beats on the door and shouts again: "What do you mean, sickly? What's going on in there? Why is no one answering me?" While his mouth flings forth these words, he thinks to himself: *I should not have let a priest come in. He must have done something . . . I took my vengeance, so why wouldn't he come and try to take vengeance for them also?*

Eyes inflamed and face shaking, Germán Alcántara Carnero begins barging the thick door with his shoulder, arm, elbow, forearm, hip, thigh, and knee, but it does not budge in the slightest, indeed this immovability was our-man's intention when, three years before, he said: "Make those doors thick and make 'em solid, make it so no one can knock 'em down. I don't want no one getting in here if they're looking to get their own back." *The window!* He turns and goes back along the passageway, thinking: *I'll climb in through the window!* Coming to the top of the stairway, he hears a strange noise behind him and halts, a buzzing and vibrating that, when he turns back, becomes a whispering. Someone is crying, or rather weeping, uncontrollably. Germán Alcántara Carnero retraces his steps, places an ear to the wood, takes in a lungful of the pestilent air seeping out through the cracks, and, hearing the priest again exclaim, "The child is sickly!" begins pounding on the door once more, the sound of his blows stirring the silent room to life. Footsteps can be heard now, a woman bathed in blood crying out, her niece crying out, and the priest muttering rosary after rosary. *I should not have let you into this house, surely you have come to take vengeance for what I did to your people*, thinks ourman, and a fire that he had thought extinguished flares up within him.

Wasn't leaving the ministry going to be the end of it? Did I not say I'd leave all my anger there? El Gringo Alcántara Carnero wonders and, sitting down on the bench in the passageway again, insists: *Did I not promise to leave the ministry and become something else? Did I not swear to no longer be that same man? How could I believe that my victims would forget?* Leaning against the wall, on the other side of which Dolores Enriqueta Celis Gómez has just given birth to Germán Camilo Alcántara Celis, ourman tries to bring his breathing and his heartbeats into step as he hears the cracked mewling of the child born a minute earlier, at 01:34 on September 28, 1960. *How could I think they wouldn't come looking for me eventually? They can do what they like with me, it's my child I care about.* Getting up again from the bench, which he stole from a hacienda nearly twenty-one years ago, Germán Alcántara Carnero bangs on the door of his room and begs: "Don't hurt them, please! Let me in, I want to see my family!" And he hears footsteps approach, a key turning, a bolt shooting back, and the lock opening.

The stout wooden panel inches open to reveal the pale and beardless face of the priest, a man no older than thirty. His eyes have the capacity to eradicate ourman's dread anytime he talks to him about his past, but fail to alleviate the fear awoken in him now. Coming out and shutting the door behind him, the priest goes over to the bench, sits, waits for ourman to do likewise, and only then speaks—words that make no sense to Germán Alcántara Carnero: "Your boy has not been born in good health. My son, there's something wrong with your child . . . " The priest's words send ourman spiraling back through time, briefly glimpsing the home in which he was born nearly sixty years ago, then the country in which he lived more or less unintentionally for a time, and the journey back from that place, the years of his reign in the Mesa Madre Buena, the day he gave it all up, the morning when he collided with the woman now moaning inside the room, the afternoon of their wedding, the breakfast at which his wife told him she was pregnant, and then the moment just a couple of minutes before, when this person standing before him pronounced the baby sickly. "What do you mean?" Germán Alcántara Carnero thunders. "What has happened to my child?" And for the first time he understands that this—a child, or, more specifically, a family—is what he was waiting for all that time, what he needed in order to break with his past.

Feigning sadness, but unable to quell the glimmer—or rather the joyful sparkle—in his eyes, the pale, beardless, and balding priest—who might in fact be in his forties—says, "My son, your child has a sickness of the bones, and your wife is not in the clear. The Lord is calling her home, let us pray that she quickly finds peace." Having failed to fully register this answer, but unable to contain or control himself, El Gringo Alcántara Carnero jumps up from the bench and wraps his enormous hands around the priest's throat. Shoving him against the wall, he roars: "What are you so happy about? Why are your eyes smiling like that? Who sent you to my home? Who sent you, you leech?" The priest, who has heard all the tales of ourman, pisses himself before he knows it; the release of liquid finds its way down his legs and into his old, worn-out boots. Germán Alcántara Carnero whispers in the man's ear, leering: "What have you done to my family, eh?" But before the priest can speak, a woman's cry bursts from the room, so distorted and painful that ourman knows something is broken, irrevocably broken, in the breast of his wife.

Tossing the priest aside, ourman pushes open the door only to be confronted with Dolores Enriqueta Celis

Gómez emitting another howl; with the vexed faces of the midwives, who a few hours earlier had given the woman a ribbon for good luck; and with his niece, whom he also pushes to one side, going straight over to the mattress on which Germán Camilo Alcántara Celis has been placed. The baby's form, head included, looks all wrong. Balling up his fists, and his stomach, too, ourman leans over, stretches out his arms, and picks up the child who, feeling hands holding him, stops crying from his misshapen mouth. Ourman turns and moves toward Dolores Enriqueta Celis Gómez, who also falls silent at her husband's approach. Coming to the bed, he holds his child out to the woman we are now watching—this woman we met for the first time just two years prior to this moment in the town square of Lago Seco and who now clutches the blue ribbon given to her by the midwife, spurning the child with a desolate look and burying her face in the pillow.

In astonishment and surprise, Germán Alcántara Carnero makes a half turn and goes back over to the mattress where he found his son. He lays the deformed body back and without pause goes out into the hallway again, where he sees the back of the priest descending the stairs. "What have you done to my family?" cries ourman, hurrying after him. "Who told you to do this to my child? Who sent you to do this to me?" He is at the top of the staircase in an instant, and kicks the priest from behind, sending him headlong down the stairs—and even as the man tumbles, eventually ending in a heap on the black flagstones, ourman demands to know: "What have you been feeding my wife these past months? What have you been doing to us all this time?" all the while torturing himself with unanswerable demands: *weren't you going to change? Weren't you going to leave everything behind and never hurt anyone again?* And the emotion that tightened around his heart ten years and eight days before this does so again now: *did you not say you would be different when you left, that you would leave all that anger behind?* Ourman hurries to the foot of the stairs, lifting the priest to his feet when he gets there. "Are you all right?" he asks, giving the priest a vacant look—the priest, paler still, blinks back at him, eventually finds the words, murmuring, "Nothing broken." He stands, blinking, before turning and going outside. He hobbles away through the garden, to where his car is parked outside the gate, and, opening the driver's door, begins to wonder why he came here at

all. For his part, Germán Alcántara Carnero, who followed him out but now turns to go back inside, wonders:
*Don't you remember what you said the day you left? Is it not
perhaps important to remember, especially considering you
have grown so stupidly fearful of late?* The car accelerates
and drives away, and ourman, crossing the plot that for
three years now he has been tilling and sowing—it will
not be long before he is the main grower of produce on
the mesa—comes inside and slams the door behind him. *I
told myself I'd do whatever it takes to forget my deeds*, Germán
Alcántara Carnero remembers, reaching the stairs, *and
what I was missing, it turns out, was this—I had to control
my anger! I had to prove I really did dump all the anger and
vengefulness at the ministry!* Distressed by his ill-shapen
son but also pleased at having controlled and contained
himself, ourman takes the steps two at a time. *So this is
how everything ends . . . I'm no longer the person I was before.
No reason for anyone to come looking for me now.*

In the hallway that leads to his room and to his family,
ourman quickens his pace, his mind once more departing from the present moment and turning to another
instant—one that underscores this present day. With no
wish to do so, Germán Alcántara Carnero observes this

other event, the one that planted the idea in him that the priest was to blame:

January 1, 1948, when the year has yet to burn away the first of its hours, and exploding fireworks continue to pepper the sky: José Ángel el Cerebro Ordóñez Sánchez and Will D. Glover exit the house they had burst into earlier on, and once they are outside hesitate over whether to take Encarnación or San Antonio. Germán Alcántara Carnero is waiting for them at the Pascua sisters' house, and they need to hurry if they are to avoid upsetting him. At the corner, El Cerebro Ordóñez—"Ordóñez the Brain," the most slow-witted of all the crew—turns and sees the lit-up windows of the house in which we find ourselves: a house with a sloping roof, a senseless feature in this part of the world, enclosed by brick walls—and clicks his tongue. He would dearly have liked to stay behind and witness the demise of Ignacio del Sagrado Sandoval-Íñiguez Martínez, the leader of the rebel group that for the past thirty years has been raising trouble on the mesa: a mesa whose principal settlement is Lago Seco: a village that is not yet a city and that houses 21,234 inhabitants, the majority of whom are believers in God but have also come to the conclusion that He is worthless.

El Cerebro Ordóñez envies the others—Manuel el
Trompo Trápaga Mora and Óscar el Chino López Ley—
whom El Gringo Alcántara Carnero told: "If you get him,
I want you to stay at the house and look after him for
me. Don't take him into the streets where people can see
him. And don't mess him up too much! Remember he's
mine." But now, having climbed into the house and tied
up the priest, they need to do something to shut him up.
El Gringo Alcántara Carnero's men are tired of listening to the priest, who launched into the psalms and the
rosary the moment he saw his captors emerging out of the
bathroom of this house and is still muttering incessantly,
even as he lies flat on the floor in front of them, bound at
ankles and wrists. Scratching his neck, El Chino, who got
this name—"the Chinaman"—because of the far-off lands
his grandparents came from to work on the train tracks
that snake through the rocky outcrop and the scrublands,
tells El Trompo to do whatever he likes as long as it shuts
him up: "Bitch is humming like a fucking beehive."

Having looked around the living room and found
nothing useful, El Trompo, who not only got this name—
"Whirligig"—because of the shape of his body—short
legs, thin hips, massive muscular torso and arms like

tree trunks—but also because once he goes into a rage there's no stopping him, goes into the kitchen and, finding a cloth on the windowsill, smiles down at the family huddling there in silence. The father is the one who betrayed Ignacio del Sagrado—who can still be heard repeating scripture in the living room. Going over to the sink, El Trompo turns on the two faucets, places a flat stone over the plughole, submerges the cloth in the water, and, lifting it out by two of its corners, rolls it into a long snake. Any moment now Ignacio del Sagrado Sandoval-Íñiguez Martínez—whom it would be better to refer to as "Delsagrado" for now—is going to start swallowing those prayers. El Trompo taps his feet as the jug in his hand fills with water, then turns off the faucets and lays the wet snake over his shoulder. He learned this trick during his time in the army, living in barracks on the border, where there was so little to occupy the men they fell in with local drug-runners—but we'll come to this later.

As El Trompo crosses the kitchen, the children who live here, whose father stares down at his hands and whose mother feigns looking up at empty air, exchange looks—bored, frightened, annoyed looks: they do not understand why four men have come into their home, why these men occupied the bathroom for most of the afternoon, why their father called out to the four men when Delsagrado came to the door, why the priest was then tied up, and why they were then told to go and sit tight in the kitchen and keep quiet.

El Trompo comes back into the living room and tells El Chino to help him get the priest up off the rug, and once they have him sitting up on a chair they bind him again, this time with a rope around his forehead. Meanwhile in the kitchen, the youngest girl is on the verge of tears but her mother turns and implores her to be quiet: "Shhh . . . shhh . . . " The same request that El Trompo is making—except that from him it is an order. "Shhh . . . shhh . . . " El Chino yanks Delsagrado's head back and El Trompo, stuffing the cloth down the priest's throat, begins pouring water after it: now Delsagrado must either swallow or drown. The priest's hands shoot outward and his legs begin to writhe like wounded snakes.

Swallowing desperately now, Delsagrado ingests a piece of the cloth and El Trompo lets go of the fabric and laughs to see the way it flops from the man's mouth, resembling the head of a bird whose neck has been wrung. "See if you go on with your praying now," says El Trompo to the wide-eyed priest. "See if you ask your god to come and save you now," he says, imitating his boss, who must be getting impatient in the house of the Pascua sisters, desperate at the lack of information, and furious at himself for sending his men alone—but we will speak of El Gringo Alcántara Carnero when we find ourselves in his presence again, given that this current moment is being recounted as it initially was told to me and that this is the only way that I—finally having discovered how to tell this story so as to clear the poison from my system—know how to narrate this tale.

"Easy," says El Chino, as El Trompo stuffs the cloth in a little more. "Screw this up and he won't be happy," he adds, just as one of the girls in the kitchen begins to wail and, farther off, in the street, a cluster of firecrackers go off. By the time the fireworks die down, the two men we are currently watching shout for someone to shut up the girl, before a single booming thud shakes the building. "What was that?" says El Chino, as he goes over to the window, opens the shutters, and sneaks a look out into the street—finding nothing but the blackness of nighttime. El Trompo opens the door and goes out, pointing toward the street corner where a group of boys are ducking behind a barrel that was once a keg and that will one day be used as a trashcan. El Chino, trembling with rage, shouts down, "Get back inside and shut the door! What do you think you're doing, idiot?" The face of the man who will one day succeed ourman at the ministry flushes red. "What do you think *you're* doing? They could be out there! Hasn't it occurred to you that they might have come?" he cries. "We don't know if they've left the Pascuas' house yet. We don't even know if Will and El Cerebro have gotten there yet."

El Cerebro Ordóñez and Will D. Glover are still racing through the streets of Lago Seco, their boss's words resounding in their ears: "Come and tell me if you got him, but be discreet. I don't want anyone using the car today. I don't want anyone coming up here shouting and screaming. It's got to look like you're out taking a nice stroll, like you're out to smell the fucking flowers."

As they do each time they receive an order from their boss, El Cerebro Ordóñez and Will D. Glover—whom we will follow now, for this was the way this story was told to me—obey. Coming to the corner of Calle Republica del 37 and Calle Candelaria and staying hidden in the mass of people, El Cerebro and Will stop outside the church in which, nearly twenty years before, Delsagrado gave the first of his incendiary sermons and, glancing at each other, try to decide whether to dive into the mass of people in the town square ahead. "Let's turn at the corner and go along Candelaria," says Will D. Glover, "then go through town from there. That's the quickest way." The two men turn left and quicken their pace, certain that their boss—who just a short while earlier cast his mind back to this memory—will be getting very anxious by now.

"It's straight all the way from here," declares Will as they pass the shop where Germán Alcántara Carnero bought a table for his house, his bed frame, and the iron trunk that adorns his workplace and of which we spoke at the beginning of this story, though we did not mention that it was Delsagrado's men he threw inside it. When they ensnare one of these men, they strip him, torture him till passing out, splash him with water to revive him, and submit him to further tortures before, having reduced each to the animal that lies inside every man, placing him inside the trunk and leaving him there for five, six, or seven days. "Come on, tell that good god of yours to come and do a little lovely miracle!" Germán Alcántara Carnero would say, enormous hands pressing shut the metal cover that will not be opened again until the man of faith is dead. Before we get to the next corner, we will pass a chandler's shop, a very large shop for yarns and threads, a mill, a butcher's shop, and a tailor's shop—the lights of which are strangely still on. Then, leaving Encarnación behind and passing a convenience store, we will glimpse the town square in the distance. At 00:34 on January 1, 1948, like every other year at this time, a town party is in full swing.

Ignoring the crowds, the booming music, and the smell of the food stalls, El Cerebro and Will D. Glover turn off Distrito and down a narrow alleyway that takes them onto Calle Magdalena, inhabited only by some pigeons picking meat from a dead rat and by three dogs tracking a small female in heat. Taking no notice of the birds that fly up as they pass, the two men we are following, convinced that they are not being watched and that their boss will be in a frenzy by now, break into a run and so, at a run, make their way along Sufragio Efectivo, Independencia, Escuinapa de Dalinas, and Reforma. They do not stop, these two men whose hearts pound as if bursting from their chests, until they notice a drunkard on the corner of Yotepec de Covarrubias.

The alcohol has emboldened him, and he watches them distastefully. Much as El Cerebro would like to stop and teach this vagrant a lesson, Will snaps his fingers, saying, "No time!" And now, here on this corner, and suddenly—as suddenly as we began following them a few minutes ago—we will leave this pair of men we have followed for several blocks, and who still have a dozen more blocks to go before they reach the Pascuas' house, where we will shortly join them again.

And so continues the dissection of this moment, which was told to me in this very way, and whose echoes Germán Alcántara Carnero will hear on the day his oldest son is born as well as eight years later, on the hour when the first of his sons will die.

At 00:51 on January 1, 1948, in the house we entered a second ago and where Amparo and Ausencia Pascua de Ramones, Juan Ignacio el Negro Romo Hernández, and Ramiro la Madrina López Palas stand in frightened silence—a silence that separates their boss's latest outburst from his next—Germán Alcántara Carnero commands that someone make him another cup of coffee and then goes to the bathroom, where, gazing down at the scintillant arc of his piss, he says to himself: "Why did you not just go yourself? Why, after all these years, would you leave it in other people's hands? What were you thinking?" But, shaking himself dry, he immediately comes back with an answer: "I needed to not be seen. The very fact I've waited so long meant I was worried he'd get away again, that someone would see me coming again and warn him."

In the kitchen of this house, a house of the same proportions as the other houses in Lago Seco—a single story with walls made of adobe bricks and of stone, rectangular in shape, with one door and three windows—Amparo Pascua, the older of the twins who live here, reheats the coffee she made earlier and has already served several times to the men in her living room. As it nears boiling point, she takes the pot off the heat and gives it a stir, then goes back into the living room, placing the steaming pot on the table, spilling a little on the previously pristine white tablecloth. Watching the fabric absorb the drops as the desert floor absorbs rainwater, Ausencia Pascua lets out a laugh: "Watch what you're doing, would you? Always dropping everything." Glaring at her twin and scraping her chair back, Amparo says, "Why didn't you go get it then, if you were so sure you wouldn't spill it?"

López Palas, aka "La Madrina" or "the Godmother" for his habit of trying to find homes for the orphans of the men and women he kills, sits down again and says in a low voice, "Shut it, you two."

Germán Alcántara Carnero enters the living room—lost in thought, his arms crossed and feet dragging—and pours himself another cup of coffee before sitting down. "Why aren't they back yet?" he half-cries, looking slowly around at the others. "What could be taking them so long?" Then, at a shout: "Where the fuck are those fuckers?" The twins and El Gringo Alcántara Carnero's underlings do not respond, leaving him to become submerged in thoughts once more: *really, what was I thinking? How could I have decided to trust those animals?* He slaps his legs, startling the others. *I should have done this differently . . . what'll I do if he slips through my hands now, and all because of my own stupid mistakes?* El Negro Romo stands up and walks over to the table, and after pouring himself a cup of coffee, feels his elbow being grabbed and shaken by ourman, knocking the cup from his hand. "How long could it take to get here?" Without a word, Amparo gets up to gather the broken cup as her sister goes into the kitchen, coming back out carrying a cloth.

"Where *are* those fuckers?" demands ourman as he steps over the twins, who are bent down cleaning up the spilled coffee, and goes over to the window: *Twenty years I spend waiting, and now I'm left waiting for those two idiots. Twenty years and all I've wanted is to be alone in a room with him, and what do I do? I let a couple of my men have him. Twenty years and when the time comes, I fuck it up!* He sees the Pascua twins reflected in the window as they go into the kitchen. *They'll see when they get here. The second they come through that door they're gonna see,* and even as he conjures these threats, Germán Alcántara Carnero castigates himself: *And what if they haven't got him? What if Delsagrado put up a fight and they had to kill him? Or if El Trompo and El Chino are turning the screw, or if they've already turned it and he's dead by the time you get there? What if they fucked up and you won't be able to get your hands on him alive?* Turning and looking around at them one at a time, ourman then turns to El Negro and La Madrina: "Get ready, we're leaving."

The two men get up from their chairs, at which moment the light bulbs flicker in their sockets: Lago Seco's power network is struggling to supply all of the town today. While the electricity supply teeters, ourman looks outside to see if the streetlamps are also wavering, but instead he sees, in the light that has begun to shine steadily again, a figure moving past the window. "Was that El Cerebro?" "I saw someone, too," murmurs Ausencia. "They're here, the bastards!" says La Madrina, pointing to the door, which someone then begins knocking on. Amparo Pascua reacts first, dashing over to the door, turning the key and pulling it open, which feels light now that our wait is over. The silhouettes of Will and El Cerebro become bodies as they step into the light, which flickers again for a moment. They are both gasping for air, but Will, leaning on the shoulder of El Cerebro, manages to say:

"We've got him . . . we tied him up in the house . . . like you said."

A smile spreads on Germán Alcántara Carnero's face and his veins throb with the excitement of a child opening presents. *So we've got him at last*, he thinks, clapping his enormous hands together.

Will, clutching the glass of water Ausencia has brought, goes on between deep, heaving breaths: "He didn't even . . . bring anyone with him . . . He wasn't expecting anything . . . You should have seen his . . . face!"

Ourman's smile broadens, creasing up his face, and a hundred noises detonate across his body, like a firebomb hurled against a wall: deep, guttural laughter first and foremost. The men and women all turn their heads, slack-jawed, fearful. They have heard their boss laugh many times before, but never like this—it is like a flock of caged birds crazily beating their wings. Stepping—or rather skipping toward them, Germán Alcántara Carnero goes over to Will and El Cerebro and, in a gesture even more shocking, gathers them up in an embrace, asking: "Did you check to make sure there was no one outside?" Then, gulping back his smile: "You had a good look around in the streets, right? And the rooftops and the cars and the bridge and the gully, and the end of Calle Caprichosa?" he insists. The two men cower: "El Trompo checked the house," says Will in a low voice, "the rest of us checked outside, a little . . . " "The thing is," says El Cerebro, "we came through town, so we couldn't have checked any of the outskirts or Caprichosa"—instantly realizing he should have kept his mouth shut.

Unfurling his arms like a vulture unfurling its wings, Germán Alcántara Carnero hurls both men to the ground and bellows: "I told you to come around the outside of town! I said not to go through the center. And why? So you wouldn't be seen, and so you could check that exit off Caprichosa!" "But we wanted to hu-hurry," says Will, frightened. "The priest didn't come as early as we thought he would, and look at the time now . . . " "We didn't want it to get even later," says El Cerebro, "we thought you'd be getting pissed." (A chuckle from the Pascua girls at this.) "You told us not to be late . . . " "But I also said I didn't want anyone seeing you coming! Didn't you stop to think why you weren't driving, or why I sent you so early?" insists ourman, flailing his hands around. "There's no way you weren't seen. No way. And someone will have gone and told his men and, since they aren't anywhere near as dumb as you two, they now know what's happened. It's all gone to fuck, and it's all your fault!" Turning and glaring at El Negro, he says: "Go out and get the car. Honk when the engine's warm. Someone's going to have come and rescued him, just you wait!" declares El Gringo Alcántara Carnero, turning back to the two men who arrived a few moments ago: "You two better hope and pray I get my revenge."

"You get ready, too. You're coming with," ourman says to La Madrina when he hears the car honking out in the street, and the two men whom we will now follow leave the house—leaving the sisters still chuckling at poor bewildered Will and El Cerebro. Germán Alcántara Carnero, pushing La Madrina into the car, takes a deep breath of the night air—the fireworks make him think of burnt gunpowder—and, getting in, slamming the door shut, bellows at El Negro to put his foot down. "If we take San Felipe," says El Negro, "it's a straight shot from here." But ourman isn't listening, he's thinking: *What if they've gone back up into the mountains? What if I don't get to lay a hand on him, again?* In Germán Alcántara Carnero's mind, the fear that he will not be able to have his revenge—a revenge he'd thought within reach—expands, becomes huge, and, in the manner of all obsessions, leaves room for nothing else.

"Hurry! Didn't you hear?" shouts ourman. He has dwelt on this particular vengeance for so many hours. "If I say put your foot down, the one and only thing I want you to do is put your fucking foot down." Germán Alcántara Carnero is a man who, for many years now, has dedicated a considerable portion of each day to conceiving of a way to torture and kill Delsagrado befitting the immensity of his anger. "It won't go any faster," says El

Negro, swerving. "But San Felipe will be quick, they've only just laid new asphalt there." The engine of the car leading us to the house where El Chino and El Trompo await accelerates, and when they're exactly halfway there, ourman glances out the window and up at the fathomless sky—the moon's brilliance engulfs that of the stars and drops a silvery layer over the mountains around the basin of the Mesa Madre Buena—and caresses the bullet he took in the chest and the chain he ripped from Delsagrado's neck several years before.

"El Negro was right," La Madrina blurts out, leaning forward from the backseat. "They repaved this whole street the other day. We'll fly there now." But though spoken directly into his ear, Germán Alcántara Carnero does not hear; he has gone back to the day when he took Delsagrado's chain from him—the same day his gun jammed and this priest put an end to Anne Lucretius Ford's life. *No gun is going to jam on me today. If he's still even there, I'm not taking any chances, I'll do the job myself.* "Nearly there yet?!" "Nearly there," says El Negro, willing the car on. "*Really* close," says La Madrina, willing it on as well.

El Negro, overcome with excitement, pushes down on the horn. "What the fuck do you think you're doing?"

rages Germán Alcántara Carnero, turning and hitting him about the head. "They could be there waiting for us. Dammit, I already told you all of this! Now there's going to be a gunfight, and it'll all end with some other bastard shooting Delsagrado down, just you wait. You'd better pray some other bastard doesn't take him down instead of me!" Rubbing his ear and pointing his chin forlornly at the couple of remaining streets, El Negro apologizes, saying: "There's no one around, though." "I don't give a shit what you think you can or can't see. Don't talk to me, and don't make a fucking peep when you pull up outside." "We better not stop right outside," says La Madrina, poking his head forward. "Why doesn't El Negro head over to the left, and we get in through the side," adds this man, but El Gringo Alcántara Carnero, one block away from his destiny now, will not be swayed. "You are going to pull up right outside, and I'm going to get out first."

Meanwhile, inside the building we recently departed, the Prieto family—father, mother, and children—along with El Trompo and El Chino, are startled by the sound of tires and a car engine out in the street. Moving furtively forward at a crouch, almost like ducks, the men who a few minutes ago knocked Delsagrado unconscious cross the living room, unholster their guns, push aside the blind with a broom handle, and peer out. "It's the boss and La Madrina!" cries El Chino. "And El Negro, too," says El Trompo, looking out as well. El Chino López stands up and unlocks the door—while El Trompo Trápaga dashes over to Delsagrado's chair to bring him round. Ourman bursts in and El Chino hastens to say: "We got him tied up in the chair. Didn't touch him after that," slams the door shut, before El Negro and La Madrina have a chance to make it in after him, and crosses the spaces in an instant. Even with Delsagrado here in front of him, he still somehow dreads losing him, all his great clouding misgivings remain—and for a moment he cannot remember the thousands of ways he has devised to end the life of this priest who rose up against the world almost thirty years ago and who rose up against him a decade after that.

Pushing past El Trompo, Germán Alcántara Carnero stops before the chair in which they have propped Delsagrado—who is still unconscious—reaches out an arm, and yanks out the cloth stuffed in Delsagrado's mouth. Delsagrado comes to feeling like his innards are being torn from him, and is met with the awful sight of ourman, who slaps him in the face with the bloody cloth before brandishing the chain hanging from his fingers. "Well now, time to find out if god is really on your side, eh? Let's even give him a minute's head start, yeah?" Beset with laughter now, Germán Alcántara Carnero swings the bullet and chain around, counting each turn: "One . . . two . . . three . . . " and so on, all the way to sixty, at which point, grinning, he takes a dagger from his other pocket and says: "But look who *has* showed up though. Look who *is* going to get a good look at your soul now . . . Or if maybe there's no such thing, eh, maybe you've been tricking everyone, maybe you've been lying to the people of this town and this plain?" Unlike in years to come—years following the tragedies that will befall the family of ourman and the woman he first encountered in the town square of Lago Seco and more recently encountered giving birth to *bornsickly*—on the day in which we currently find ourselves, January 1, 1948, Germán Alcántara Carnero does not believe in the existence of a soul, or indeed in any sort of afterlife aside from the prospect of his body being feasted on by worms. He does not believe these things because at this moment, as the sun rises over this very high plain on which we find ourselves, he has not had his life and his beliefs shaken, or rather upturned, by the deaths of those dearest to him, deaths he may not escape by simply upping and leaving, as he did after the death of his youngest sister in his youth.

An unexpected calm descends on ourman as he flicks open the knife and begins admiring the blade. Speaking softly—"Let's see if it's in there, why don't we, if you showed up today with your soul"—he chuckles and, flipping the knife around, plunges the blade into Delsagrado's throat. Delsagrado blanches, and he begins to shake, eyes swiveling around, and a series of incomprehensible coughing noises issuing from his mouth. "Something you wanted to say?" Germán Alcántara Carnero says in his best mocking voice, before glancing up at his men and then grabbing the priest by the hair, pulling the blade from his trachea and, raising it high, plunging it back in once more—once, twice, again and again and again. And though Delsagrado has begun to convulse, he manages to speak a few words that rob ourman of his smile. "What's that? How dare you speak of her!" The priest, who will be dead in a few lines, smiles or tries to smile and, mustering all of his own rancor, thrusts his own particular dagger into the very core of ourman, who registers with astonishment the pernicious last words of Ignacio del

Sagrado Sandoval-Íñiguez Martínez: "Again a woman . . . an end . . . a day . . . a child. A family . . . starting after . . . after . . . " Separating the head, still spewing blood, from the rest of the body, Germán Alcántara Carnero hears something out in the street and, ashen, barks at his men: "Ready yourselves, you two, we're leaving."

Then, watching his men go over to the door, he repeats: "Again a woman . . . an end . . . a day . . . a child. A family . . . starting after . . . after . . . " He repeats the words, feeling that, with them, Delsagrado has somehow succeeded in violating Anne L. Ford once more, this time with words he will remember for the rest of his days—though they will take on an entirely different meaning on the still-distant afternoon when the first of his children is born—the afternoon, that is, in which this chapter began.

DISAPPEARANCE, ESCAPE

MAY 27, 1911, and another knot in our account of this life—a knot in which, at the hour when the sun beats down on the backs of men across the Mesa Madre Buena and the earth succumbs to the drowsiness and slowness that succeed spring, Germán Alcántara Carnero hears a sudden whistle and stops swinging his mattock. Puzzled, ourman, still a boy at this point in our story, turns and gazes over his shoulder, and when the whistle cuts through the air again, the three mangy dogs that were sleeping on the ground nearby rouse themselves, sniffing the air for a smell that is yet to reach the boy— the smell of a smudge coming down over the scrubland, where the heat from the earth meets the heat dropping from the incandescence that is the sky at this time of year.

He looks at the horizon, which is very clear, and sees the smudge as it continues to advance over the scrub. *It's been so long since we've had any kind of wind*, thinks Germán Alcántara Carnero. *Two, maybe three weeks and not the tiniest gust*, he thinks, casting his mind back as the smudge continues its approach, gradually growing into a silhouette. The whistling man whistles again, calling to attention the men, women, and children hereabouts, who all leave off their work and, like Alcántara Carnero, stand and wait. The local landowner—the lord and master, that is, of these lands and of all the people in them—approaches on his mare, a thousand swirling starlings following in his wake. A solitary cloud crosses the sun—brief respite for Germán Alcántara Carnero as he wonders what orders they're about to be given.

The cloud's fleeting shadow, as fleeting as the words I am writing here, moves across the plowed field, across the plots in which seeds have already been sown, and then over the path along which the horse—whose glinting owner we will refer to as *lordandmaster*—is trotting. Eye drawn by the glints coming off of lordandmaster's clothes, ourman—whom we will be better off calling *ouryoungman*, though in truth he isn't even quite a young man yet—does not notice his dogs rousing themselves until they set to barking. "Quiet, you three!" he says as the lordandmaster whistles again. But the dogs continue to bark and whine, and, leaning down, he kicks one of the beasts in the neck and the other on the snout: "I said quiet!"

A little way off, ouryoungman hears someone asking: "What's he want?" It is the man who always speaks up when anything happens in these parts: "What is it this time?" Another peon, a few meters from us, answers with a laugh: "He's come to hand out some presents." All those in earshot laugh. "He's here to give us his horse." And the first man, plunging his machete into the soil and wiping his brow, says: "I bet he's going to tell us to all go home. I know him, and I know he don't like being out in the hot sun like this . . . Bet he's going to tell us, 'Whoever doesn't stay home will pay . . . ' Look at him, so sure of himself—cock of the walk!"

Lordandmaster whistles once more—not because any of his workers haven't heard him already, but simply because he can, and because he knows it annoys these men.

"He's frightened it'll start here, too!" says the man who has begun exhorting his companions. "Frightened we'll rise up as well. Bet you he's going to come and complain about those ten men, and warn us off joining them." "I wish he was afraid!" says one of the older men—the one who's been working for longest on these lands, lands where the punishing heat even seeps through the ground, quickly fermenting any recently buried bodies. The man who spoke first, undeterred, indifferent to the old man's reply, takes three steps forward and says: "He's come to say, 'woe to those thinking of welcoming them into their homes.'" But again, ouryoungman doesn't hear this. He has just noticed a strange insect crawling from the ear of his dog and trying to pick it off. Seeing its blue-green wings, Germán Alcántara Carnero thinks: *It's a Jerusalem Cricket. I'll give it to María, she'll like it*. He reaches out a hand, but then feels a sharp pain, a heavy blow that, though it doesn't touch him, cuts the insect in two and therefore hurts him nonetheless. "That bug don't bite, but he does!" says one of the peons as he comes by, pointing to lordandmaster at the far end of the field. "Better get over there now."

Germán Alcántara Carnero watches in anger as the man, the machete in his hand, walks grudgingly over, but then falls in behind him. When he reaches the group surrounding lordandmaster, he catches the tail end of a phrase: " . . . I will go and seek them out, personally, and I will find them, and I will mete out such punishment on each and every one." With his outsize hands, Germán Alcántara Carnero forces open a space between the men, who now turn their heads to the north, where the man who killed his insect has begun speaking: "So go back to our houses, is that it? And once we get there stay put? I have a better idea—why don't you and your family go to fuck?" The men, though already silent, fall quieter still, and ouryoungman braces himself: lordandmaster immediately crosses the circle, his hand reaching for his gun, which he levels at the man's head and, still advancing, pulls the trigger. And the man who killed the insect is blown onto his back.

The mouth of the fallen man issues the final gurgling sounds that his body will ever emit, as though his heart and lungs, before giving in, had to unleash a final insult to the workers looking on in silence, heads bowed, waiting for their next order. "Home," roars lordandmaster, "all of you get home, and don't let me catch any of you going out." They all stare back at him, all except for Germán Alcántara Carnero, who is watching the hole through which the dead man's brains are dribbling out. "Don't none of you come back out again till I say so." And with that, lordandmaster mounts his mare once more and, pulling hard on the reins, shouts: "Don't let me hear that any of you have been talking with the Rio Verde men, nor showing them any kind of hospitality." Pleased with their silence and with the obedient turning and walking away of his workers—men who, even with their backs to him, don't dare to defy him in words or thought— lordandmaster spins and begins moving off, but then ouryoungman's dogs begin barking again and he turns back. *What's Félix's boy doing now?* he wonders, with confusion that will soon produce a smile on his face. *What's he doing peering at the dead man? Is he really going to . . . ?* Nodding his head, captivated, lordandmaster lets out a laugh as he sees the person who will one day be ourman reach out and thrust his outsize fingers into the bloody wound. Lordandmaster, up on his mare, applauds, saying to himself: *This you'll never forget, not this, Félix's little boy,* before tugging on the reins again and setting off. The surprise on the face of ouryoungman—the only worker remaining—lingers: he has seen dead men before but never gone so far as to touch one, and never imagined the blood would be this warm. Crouching, looking in the dead man's eyes, he whispers: "That's what you get, fucker, for hurting my beetle. It was meant to be a gift."

He looks up, the only things around him now his three dogs and the vultures that have just landed a little way off—beyond them across the fields he can see the diminishing silhouettes of the workers picking their way through the scrub, and beyond that the rocky outcrop, sandstone winking in the sun, and beyond the rocky outcrop the vast swath of thicket land where his family lives and where a dam will one day be erected.

Picking his way across the fresh furrows to his mattock, he gathers it up along with the two halves of the beetle that crawled out of his dog's ear, and thinks of his sister, who turns fourteen today and who has never uttered a word in her life: she was born with a tongue the wrong size for her mouth. "I'll find her something else. By the time I get back to the house, I swear I'll have another present." Scanning the horizon once more, ouryoungman enjoins his dogs—who are casting resigned looks at the fly-covered corpse also being contemplated by the jumpy vultures: "Come on, you three. Let's go!" Leaving the field behind and passing up and down a number of small knolls, he cuts into the part of the land where at certain times of the year beanstalks and at others alfalfa and sorghum and grass and corn grow, in haphazard manner: a manner replicated by almost everything on this plain and thus by this story as well. Here a hundred shoots, there a group of stalks and the heads of some maize, and over there, corncobs in an unlikely line. Here the earth begins to change: the weeds begin to break up into discrete clumps, drifting farther apart and soon coming to resemble islands and then finally small islets charting a course in an ocean of earth—on the surface of which the stone just thrown by Germán Alcántara Carnero lands.

Without breaking stride, ouryoungman leans down and plucks another stone from the path, cleaning the soil from it as he did the previous stone—spitting on it and rubbing it with both hands before carefully checking it over and then hurling it angrily toward the horizon. He has no choice but to find a new gift for María del Sagrado Alcántara Carnero. On this part of the path we are on, where the soil turns sharp and rough underfoot and even the islets of clumped grass desist, the boy who will one day be ourman is more likely to find the surprise he's looking for: a stone with a fossil inside, one that shows how this area was submerged beneath water in epochs past. He bends down, picks up another stone, checks it, discards it. At the point the path exits the stretch of seemingly ravaged lands and enters the area that precedes the rocky outcrop we are very soon to arrive in—a place where the ground resembles leprous skin—Germán Alcántara Carnero leans down again and, picking up a fourth stone, smiles and gives a small excited skip. Finally, a good gift.

Loose stones crunch beneath his feet as he quickens his pace. His sister is going to explode in happiness when she sees it, he knows she will. She'll howl and tremble and clap her hands, though none of the claps will connect. Hurrying along, twenty meters shy now of the rocky swath of land with glasslike edges we saw winking earlier on in the distance—where the sun plays on the twisting tracks that in turn offer up their thin, rusted iron veins—this scalding barren stretch—a scurrying, scrabbling sound turns our heads as well as that of the boy: a lizard has shot beneath a couple of slabs of obsidian. Then a screech from above makes him look up: in the sky, a strange glowing ring finally makes the sun the center of something. The sight of this white hoop and the position assumed by the sun prompt the thought: *It'll still be light when I get home,*

I'll be able to give her—the cripple girl he sleeps next to and whom he comforts when she cries—*two surprises*.

Hurrying his dogs along, he moves forward over ground that no longer crunches but that screeches like nails scraping on glass. Halfway across this rocky tract there is a sea of silicates upon which basalt rock, obsidian, and igneous rocks, spewed up by the earth thousands of years ago, float like corks. This current stretch of the path is a kind of upside-down sky, gleaming and glinting. In a bare black triangle of earth where the path forks, a couple of opossums appear, and the dogs, baying, fly after them. After a short chase, bones are being crunched and flesh and fur torn apart: the male got away but not the female, nor the nine babies she was carrying, which the hounds also gulp down. They fight over the remains of the mother: one tries to makes off with the spine, another with one of the ears, and the other with one of the still-twitching paws. "That's enough!" When they ignore him and go on eating, he picks up a large rock, goes over, and with a shout brings it down on the head of one of the trio—its forelegs buckle and it lets out a howl.

The wounded dog totters away from him across the rocks, trying to scrape its own head with its paws, and, like the two dogs that escaped the boy's fury, looks up at his master when he says: "I said enough! We've got to go!" Hounds in tow, Germán goes back to the fork in the path, taking the left path and gathering the mattock he placed on the ground, a tool he was given by his father—who, condemned not just by the state of his thyroids but also by the diabetes that has recently begun gnawing at his hands, has had to resort to using his forearms whenever he wishes to give his son a beating—Germán—who has for a long while now been his father's match and could take him on if he wanted to, only the thought has not yet occurred to him—again quickens his pace, calling for the dogs to do the same. The path curves east and then east again, and then it seems to veer to the west, coming up a slight incline and out of the ocean of quartzes, obsidians, and anthracites, before leaving behind the carpet of crystal and slate and the noises made by Germán's feet on the glass and the reflections that slash back and forth across the space like daggers. Behind the boy comes the mute procession of his hounds: the oldest, followed by the most intelligent, followed by the one with bloody snout and skull.

Just where the ground turns soily once more, Germán, though giving no great thought to the strange sensation swelling in his gut, and though unsure why his insides are teeming, stops to wait for the injured animal. Wheezing with every footstep, its tail continues to wag a little as it approaches. It reaches Germán, who has knelt down, and it lies down, letting out a few yelps as the boy's two huge hands stroke it and scruff it about the neck and head. The boy wipes the blood from the pelt with his shirt, and says into a very large ear: "It wasn't me who hurt you, boy. I didn't drop that stone. I could never hurt you." Getting to his feet again with a leap, he spurs his dogs home and then notices his hands are covered in blood. He smiles to himself, very excited: *I'll tell my sister about this, too—not just her gift, but the insect, the whistling, the machete, the boss coming down and giving orders, that guy complaining, the hole in his head, the warm blood, his brain, oh, and the way it smelled so bad.*

He's advanced another ten or so meters by the time the dog gets up and, licking its front paws a couple of times, falls in behind the other two. But before it can walk five paces it halts, arches its back, opens its maw as wide as it will go, and vomits up two of the baby opossums; these it sniffs for a moment, licking at them, and then, after a moment, ingesting them for a second time. After this the dog shakes itself and, revived, lets out a bark and sets off along the path on either side of which we now see, as well as the clumps of mesquite and acacia that have lately begun growing hereabouts, two very large cacti, one agave, a kidneywood tree, and six bishop's weed plants. We are suddenly in the thicketland. Hurrying on, Germán drops his head for a moment, looks at his lengthening but still not very long shadow, and thinks of the hours left in the day. He'll play with María for the rest of the afternoon and evening, maybe they'll even go down to the crater. *And if Heredí gives me a hand, we could go and have a look at the tracks.* The thought of the train excites ouryoungman, knowing how much María loves it, how thrilling she finds the noise and the rumble of the passing carriages.

And there it is now—beyond the tall tattered kidney-wood, beyond the spread of cacti and the horizontal black pepper tree felled by lightning a couple of years ago, just where the soil turns ash-black: the shack in which he lives with his two sisters and his parents. Breaking into a run, he who will one day be ourman is thirty meters from the shack when he catches sight of his mother and the sister for whom he has not brought a present. In the ensuing three or four paces he expects to see María appear in the doorway, but no: just his mother and the other sister holding hands, and beyond them the shack and the abandoned chicken coop and the tall fig tree he climbs at night. Ouryoungman immediately senses something, he doesn't know what, and his dogs begin to bark—very rare for them upon returning to the shack.

"What are María's clothes doing there?" he says to the woman as his dogs begin to bay. "Where's my sister?" Though deaf, his mother knows he's asking after María, and, spreading her arms wide, hacks up a strange sobbing noise before collapsing to the floor. "I said where is she?" Heredí de los Consuelos Alcántara Carnero cowers behind her mother. Stepping over them, he runs to the shack, and, throwing aside the ragged cloth over the doorway, finds his father sprawled on the ground, looking somehow leonine.

"What have you done with her?" He drops his tools on the floor, seeking out his father's eyes with his own, the blind one and the seeing one, both of which now come to settle on his son. "Where's my fucking sister?" Leaning down, ouryoungman reaches for a brick hod and, without stopping to think, raises it high above his head and advances on Félix Salvador. "You'll never find out," sneers the father, waving the two gnarled stumps that were once hands: "Let's see if you can guess! Go on, tell me what you think's happened to her!" Ouryoungman, unable to contain himself, steps forwards and lashes his father across the face with the hod. The older man shields himself with his armstumps, but he fails to protect his mouth and his teeth, which his son, raising the hod once more, smashes with a second blow. An arc of blood splashes down over the man's jowls and the pair of flaccid tits.

Casting around for something, anything he can bring down on his father's head, overcome by a desire to bury the man under all the objects formerly used to instill terror in the family, he grabs a couple of canes and hurls them at him, then some planks of wood lying on the floor, various stones, a metal beam, a couple of effigies of the Virgin and Baby Jesus, a broken bench, three bottles, and a pot that smashes on contact with his father's motionless form. Dispirited, overwhelmed, but with his blood still up, Germán Alcántara Carnero leaves his home, beckons his dogs with a wave of the hand, crosses the yard without a word to Heredí, and marches straight out into the rocky outcrop. Soon, tired from all the walking and from thoughts of what he has done, he will fall asleep on the ground, later to be found, woken, threatened, beaten, and ultimately taken in by a group of young men who will then induct him into an army that will become his ticket out of this place—all things that will happen with us no longer present to witness them.

Halting in the doorway of the shack, we watch Germán receding in the distance, a silhouette, then a blur like the blur we glimpsed at the opening of this chapter, and we then, too, take our leave of this place and of this moment, traveling forward in time to a moment when the name "ouryoungman" has been supplanted by the nickname "El Gringo." There he is, El Gringo, propped on his elbows on the ground, drinking and chatting with Camilo Mónico Macías Osorio, El Demónico, recounting the day he left home: "Then I saw a great flock of blackbirds fly up, and I knew my little sister was dead. And I lay down and slept." And before he can say: "It was then that the five of them found me," El Gringo Alcántara sees two balls of fire coming at him and jumps to his feet. He is now as tall as he ever will be, though he is yet to fully flesh out as a man.

He spits out the drink and throws the bottle aside while trying to clear his drunken thoughts. It is then that he realizes that the two howling, zigzagging torches are his two remaining dogs (the oldest, the one that was present the day of his birth he buried three years ago now, high in the sierra). "Who's done this!" screams El Gringo Alcántara Carnero. "What the fuck is this?" He moves away from the bonfire around which three of the Díaz Cervantes brothers let out deep, guttural laughs. Macario, Pedro, and Baldomero know very well it was Demetrio who set fire to the dogs. "If only you'd run like that a week ago!" shouts Baldomero Díaz Cervantes. "We would have had to burn you, too!" says Macario. For a week now, Germán Alcántara Carnero, the Díaz Cervantes brothers, and El Demónico Macías Osorio— who for four years have been part of the troop whose campfires currently dot a large portion of the hillside— have been a tight group, an unbreakable brotherhood, looking out for each other, even putting the others before themselves.

But on July 24, 1917, six days before this moment in which the burning, screaming dogs run around trailing columns of smoke and cinders, Germán Alcántara

Carnero broke this brotherhood by handling a very delicate moment very clumsily: Jacinto Díaz Cervantes and El Gringo Alcántara Carnero separated from the others to go and scout the higher ground, and stumbled on a couple of large watering holes. "Must be geysers," said Jacinto, excited. "What's a geyser?" asked ouryoungman, puzzled. "Can I drink the water?" With a laugh, dropping his carbine rifle and his knife on the ground, Jacinto said: "What you can do is bathe in it." And the oldest of the brothers that had found Carnero six years before removed his threadbare garments and proceeded to dive into the water.

Gathering up Jacinto's weapons and glancing about like a rabbit leaving its warren, El Gringo Alcántara Carnero—who was given this nickname because since learning that there were countries other than his own in the world, he'd been swearing over and over to someday go and settle in one of them—approached the water's edge and hissed: "Come on, leave it. It's hot as hell round here." The oldest of the five Díaz Cervantes boys just splashed some water at him and let out a laugh before diving down. Surfacing, he laughed: "Come on, dive in. You've seen as well as I have there's nobody around."

Germán Alcántara Carnero barked: "We aren't here to splash around. They told us not to be too long." With a hard look, Jacinto Díaz Cervantes groaned at the young man he had looked after and schooled for the past six years. "Since when do you raise your voice at me? I'll get out when I damn well want to!"

Before El Gringo Alcántara Carnero could answer the de facto leader of their small group, they both heard the thump of footsteps and the unmistakable sound of men's voices. "Here, my things!" said Jacinto, half-shouting—trying to shout quietly. He turned and began swimming toward the edge—he was fifteen or twenty meters out by now. Our young man looked down at the rifle and the knife in his hands and, taking a few steps backward, said: "This is what you get for not listening to me—for never listening to anyone." The approaching voices were already very near, and the oldest Díaz Cervantes, seeing there was no chance of escape, stopped swimming and simply glared at El Gringo Alcántara Carnero as he turned and crept off in the direction of their camp. And when he got there none of the brothers could bring themselves to believe the story ouryoungman had hurriedly concocted, leading them, six days later, on July 30, 1917, moments before we arrived at this current knot, to put a match to both of his dogs.

"I heard them say it was Demetrio, and then they said we should've burned you alive, too!" exclaims El Demónico Macías Osorio as he catches up with Germán Alcántara Carnero, panting and sweating from having run for a mile behind the two balls of fire that, even as the flames consumed them, had stayed close to each other. Kneeling on the ground, Carnero is embracing what remains of his dogs. "I couldn't even hold them properly at the end! I couldn't even touch them." "I told you," says El Demónico, who's had running disagreements with his brothers for months, "we shouldn't have stayed on. Without Jacinto, those four are a piece of shit." "Where are those bastards now?" says the young man who will one day be ourman, pushing away the hands that have just helped him to his feet. "They'll be up there waiting for us," El Demónico whispers, as he brings Alcántara Carnero close, keeping him from running straight off. "Instead of heading up there, why don't we drop down and go after Demetrio? It was him who lit them up." Ouryoungman, a little calmer now, kneels next to the two scorched corpses, silently promising them vengeance. Then, to El Demónico: "All right, we go after Demetrio."

The soldiers, in large groups around their fires, watch as Germán Alcántara Carnero and El Demónico come running past. Some offer condolences—they know how dear his dogs were to him—while others make the sign of the cross. The Milky Way is visible in the night sky, scored by the halting tracks of fireflies.

"Take my gun if you want," says El Demónico when he sees that El Gringo Alcántara Carnero is unarmed—he set off running without taking anything. "Or my knife?" "The knife, give me the knife," says ouryoungman, reaching back like a runner reaching for a baton. Feeling its hilt in his hand, he quickens his pace, drawn on by a clear, striking premonition, turning onto the very track taken by Demetrio Díaz Cervantes minutes before. Coming past a thick clump of high grasses and ducking under a very tall agave, he picks up on the sound of panting, of heaving lungs—a snorting, almost—that gives away the man running up ahead. They stop: the sound is coming closer. "Who else is going to be hurrying anywhere at such an hour?" hisses El Gringo, answering El Demónico's question before he has even spoken it.

Germán Alcántara Carnero leaps at Demetrio Díaz Cervantes the moment he emerges, and the pair tumble down the slope, knees, elbows, and hips cracking against stones and boulders as they go. Several meters lower down, the pair we are now watching struggle to their feet, and ouryoungman realizes he has dropped the knife; his adversary brandishes a long blade. "Let's see if you've got the balls," says Demetrio Díaz Cervantes as they begin to circle each other, "to take on a man who isn't in the water. We got our hands on one of the Federal soldiers who killed Jacinto today, and a while back we found his knife among your things . . . " At this, the second oldest Díaz Cervantes brother squints and throws himself at ouryoungman with a snarl. In a single, unexpected movement—an unexpected sideways-forward jump— Germán Alcántara Carnero avoids the blow and, rapid and assured, knocks Demetrio to the ground, before disarming him and kneeling on his chest. Flinging away the knife, El Gringo Alcántara Carnero says: "I don't need your knife and I don't need to throw you in the water. I don't even need to set you on fire."

His two enormous fists begin pummeling Demetrio's face and head, while he shouts down at him: "I couldn't even touch them! I didn't even get to hold them before they died!" Jumping to his feet, he begins kicking Demetrio about the ribs and stamping on his battered head, shouting all the while: "They were innocent—why'd you have to hurt them?" Looking down at the head, a bloody mess by now, Carnero becomes aware of a second yoke, one that has weighed on him for a long time, and is reminded of the one he removed from his back seven years earlier, and the dead man whose bloody head he thrust his fingers into comes to mind, and now, now that the memories are under way, he cannot stop them, he sees again the moment he arrived back at his house, his mother's guilt-ridden look and the empty eyes of little Heredí de los Consuelos, the violence he inflicted on his father, leaving the house where he was born, meeting the brothers Díaz Cervantes . . . *If they hadn't picked me up, I'd surely have gone back and looked for her . . .* "If you five hadn't *kidnapped* me," he growls, "I'd never have gone off without her."

After kicking Demetrio Díaz Cervantes, harder, harder, El Gringo finally stops, falls quiet, and is still for a moment before leaning down and taking the prostrate body by the neck. He lifts Demetrio up so that their eyes are level—though Demetrio's have fallen shut. *I'm going to have to make another getaway today!* thinks he who will very soon become ourman, placing his hands, seemingly made for such a task, around the throat of Demetrio Díaz Cervantes, and proceeding to strangle the life out of him.

"We need to get away before the brothers come looking." And with that the pair head down the mountainside—Germán Alcántara Carnero guessing at the terrain in the dark, hastening El Demónico Macías forward—who stops every so often for air. They make their way down a long, steep scarp and head along a ravine. *So!* thinks Germán Alcántara Carnero, *turns out there was a worse way to leave a place!* And at the point when he places a foot in the river, we cease following these two young men, who are soon to be enveloped by the night, and, as Alcántara Carnero cries: "Into the water! That way they can't track us!" we move in a direction that in fact puts distance between us and the moment when I become a character in this story. The rest of this escape we will not see: the knots contained in this chapter have been untied and now the only things that matter are the story of a person dear to ourman who choked, and the bullet that one day struck ourman in the chest—the two knots that follow this barren blank space:

CONVERSION, FORSAKING

THE ESCAPE THROUGH THE RAVINE is followed by these moments: a moment, three quarters of the country and a little more than fifty years away, that concludes with Germán Alcántara Carnero's bloody chest, and with him offering his trinket to another person. This person being the one who at 07:26 on October 12, 1968, is rolling around on the ground gasping for air. Six minutes are still to transpire before we see El Gringo Alcántara Carnero come in and offer his bullet and chain to this deformed young man, currently lying on the floor—the same deformed young man whose birth occasioned a priest's cry: "Sickly! The baby has been born sickly!" This

young man, really no more than a boy—and he won't
live to become a man—has accepted a challenge from
his siblings and cousins, who have taunted him with the
words: "Can't you swallow it whole?"

First though, a short while before, at 07:13, when
daylight makes mirrors of the windows and splashes
violets and reds on the adobe mud walls, and as sparrows
and mockingbirds begin their chattering, and Germán
Camilo's cousins and his two brothers, Enriqueta and
Alonso Alcántara Celis, and Ramiro, José Julio, and
Mariangeles Celis Comesaña, give up playing in the
deserted garden—a place where the break of day acts as
a warning: time to go home.

The gradual drawing away of the darkness and of the
silence, which elsewhere in Lago Seco mark the beginning
of children's games, here means the end of any such fun.
Germán Alcántara Carnero has forbidden his children
and nephews and nieces from playing after bornsickly
wakes, which is why they have developed the habit of
getting up at night, why they have been chasing one
another around for the past two hours, and why they
ought now to be going inside. But today the five of them
have not gone inside at the appointed hour, and rather

than slinking home in single file they advance in a rowdy circle, their raised voices breaking another of the rules laid down by ourman.

"Stop shouting, we don't want them to see us!" Enriqueta cries.

"I'm not shouting!" declares José Julio: "*He* lost!"

To which Alonso Alcántara Celis says: "You didn't even touch me—how can I have lost?"

These voices rain down over the scrubland, one falling on the house that ourman ordered be constructed twelve years ago.

"I don't care who won!" insists little Enriqueta Alcántara Celis. And then, even louder: "Stop shouting, let's go in now!"

It occurs to none of them that their raised voices are raining down on the house—"Why won't you accept it? You know you're lying." "*You're* the liar!" "No, *you're* the liar!"—and have indeed awoken bornsickly. The group we are watching is no longer being watched by us alone, as bornsickly drags himself over to his bedroom window and, seeing them crossing the parched garden, he begins to melt with excitement, like an ice cube melts when placed on the floor. Beneath the poorly tended lawn lies the memory of the ruts and furrows made here more than half a century ago by El Gringo Alcántara Carnero when he worked the land with mattock, scythe, and trowel.

"You didn't get anywhere near him!" yelps Mariangeles Celis Comesaña, leaping across a dip in the earth, just as bornsickly brings his face up to the window, and as Alonso Alcántara Celis, who wants an end to the matter, cries: "You didn't even catch up with me. You've *never* caught me. So how could you have got me?"

The voices carry to the door of the bunkerlike house before us, transpiercing the windows—ourman wakes with a start, and can immediately tell that it isn't his wife's voice he's hearing. For eight years now, ever since the day the priest imparted the news of his son's birth and his son's ailment, the woman we first met in the town square of Lago Seco has lived inside the pages of the book she now sits holding in her hands, a volume in which, every now and again, she comes across a story that fills her withered soul with hope once more, a passage or phrase that seems to contain some speck of absolution.

El Gringo sits up with a frown, cracks his aching neck, swings his legs over the side of the bed—his hips and lower back also creaking, cracking, and popping.

He thinks to himself: *It's against the rules, and they know it.* Ourman is utterly tired—bornsickly's never-ending weeping has worn him down in these intervening years—but the sounds of the children's voices immediately rouses him, and he hurtles across the room. "Still out there?" he cries, while hoping, though not feeling hopeful, that bornsickly might not have been awoken. Throwing open the curtain, he feels Dolores's bony hand grip his shoulder—but before she can say "Can I read you a little of my book?" he has already given his answer: "First I have to deal with those children of yours."

A few meters outside the door, where the garden—which, were it not for the presence of the children, would be overrun by plants and quiet as a cemetery—drops down into a small cobblestone patio, Enriqueta and Alonso Alcántara Celis, and Ramiro, José Julio, and Mariangeles Celis Comesaña hear a sound, and look up in unison: El Gringo Alcántara Carnero is at his bedroom window banging on the frame: the window itself no longer opens, its frames having long ago melted and fused under the punishing sun. "Piece of shit window," hisses ourman as he continues to bang on the frame, while at his back Dolores Enriqueta Celis Gómez, whose left arm bears the ribbon she was given upon the birth of her first child, insists: "I want to read you this part—let me read it to you before you go down." Ignoring her, glaring down at the children, El Gringo Alcántara Carnero repeats inwardly: *They must've woken him up . . . I hope at least he hasn't made it to his window.* Ourman brings his fist down on the window frame once more, which, as distressed by the sun as Dolores Enriqueta Celis Gómez has been by the lack of it, splinters, coming clean off its hinges.

El Gringo Alcántara rests his hands on the flaking sill, hears without hearing his wife stubbornly repeat herself: "It's just a short passage," while in his pupils—once black, now shadowy—the frightened children are reflected. A barked whisper: "How many times do I have to tell you?" All at once the children begin hissing apologies, saying they weren't really out playing, really they weren't . . . but El Gringo Alcántara doesn't want to know: "Get inside now! And don't let him see you!"

Meanwhile, as the children hurry forward across the cobbled courtyard, inside his room bornsickly loses his balance and topples to the floor: he twists and writhes, his attempts to get up like those of an overturned turtle.

Inside the sturdy, warrenlike house, the others' hatred for ourman and for his firstborn—his favorite, the one he lives for—comes pouring forth: "It isn't fair that we don't get to go out." "I wish he was dead!" "Who cares if he sees us?" "Why should he mind?"

"What if we asked him to come and play with us?"

At this they stop and look at one another.

A noise drops from above them: Germán Alcántara Carnero is dragging a chair across the cement and placing it in front of his wife's chair, where, having shut the blinds, she sat down a moment ago with a sudden shout: "Come here, now!" Then, smiling: "I'm going to read to you of our salvation!"

Still trying to get up, bornsickly hears this, too, following by his father's grumbles and then by footsteps approaching his door: his cousins and siblings have thought up a game.

El Gringo Alcántara Carnero sits sullenly, saying to himself: *You ought to be downstairs . . . there's no way he's still asleep . . .*

His wife, stretching out the arm that bears the stained ribbon she was given the day of the birth and that she has not taken off since, turns on the desk lamp, the faint light pushing back the darkness as the Alcántara Celis couple, whose oldest child trembles to hear the voices on the other side of his door, look at each other for a brief moment: both briefly letting down their guards after eight years of indifference, disappointment, and resentment.

In the hallway below, meanwhile, bornsickly is being lifted off the floor and taken through into the kitchen. Bornsickly, a child who has never developed properly, is little more than an enormous head, a torso the shape and size of an old toaster, and four stubby limbs. Ramiro Celis Comesaña, the oldest of ourman's nephews, props bornsickly up on his two deformed legs. He looks like a lump of clay that has been crushed in someone's hand, in much the same way bornsickly now crushes the peach given to him by Mariangeles Celis Comesaña. "Don't give him anything yet!" cries Enriqueta Alcántara Celis, seeing what her cousin has done: "Who told you we'd started yet?" she adds, putting half an avocado, three lemons, and a knife into the pail that her brother and cousins are also filling up. "Clean his hand off now . . . when have you ever seen a cripple with filthy hands like that?" says Ramiro Celis Comesaña, and instantly his eyes widen to the size of plates: bornsickly has put the crushed peach into his mouth and swallowed it in one go.

Laughing like they have not laughed in a long time, the cousins and children of ourman—who is still in his room inwardly demanding that his wife get on with it—entertain themselves by stuffing more and more things into bornsickly's mouth: a lemon cut in four, a crushed guava, half a sausage, three cloves of garlic. The giggles have turned to howls of laughter, the children's original idea for a game forgotten.

You ought to be down there by now . . . what if something's happened to him?

Spurred by the flare of yearning in her stomach and the hope, not yet entirely extinguished, that they might finally find peace, Dolores Enriqueta, little interested in ourman's glowering demeanor, readjusts the camisole she has not washed in a number of months, crosses her legs, lets out a long sigh, and begins, haltingly, to read:

"Saul, who had conserved the vestments in which Saint Sebastian was stoned, was an Israelite who had been born in Tarsus, the capital of Cilicia. By birth he was a citizen of Rome and, this being so, as well as his

Hebrew name, he had a Roman one: Paul. His parents, Jews hailing from the lands of Benjamin, were Pharisees, and it was in this environment that the boy was raised . . . "

"What was that noise?" ourman suddenly asks, but his wife is not listening:

"At a very young age he was taken to Jerusalem to complete his studies in the school of Gamaliel, a teacher renowned for his mastery of science and for the serious-ness of his ways. A passionate Pharisee, loyal to the sect that had taught him everything, Saul abhorred Christians and . . . "

"It sounded like a cry to me . . . " insists Germán Alcántara Carnero, but still his wife goes on:

"His hate for the Christians grew and grew, until reaching unexpected extremes; no longer was he content to persecute them in Jerusalem, but his furious zeal led him to . . . "

"There's that cry again . . . Now they're all shouting . . . "

"Once he had reached a position of power, he put himself forward to transport as many Christian men and women in chains to Jerusalem . . . And this was why, on his way to Damascus, Saul's mind was on torments and the meting out of justice . . . "

"Really, they're all shouting . . . " cries Germán Alcántara Carnero, jumping to his feet. "Have you gone deaf, or do you just not want to hear?" He dashes over to the door. "Listen, they're shouting our names!"

Pushing open the bedroom door, Germán Alcántara Carnero goes down into the passageway and shouts: "What's going on?" while upbraiding himself inside: *You should have gone down before . . . what if something's happened to the one you love as much as you loved your little sister?*

The confusion of cries coming from the kitchen reach the passageway mixed together and the voice of womanwhopreaches, who in her room has already gone into a trance and grows quieter: "And he trembling and astonished said . . . Lord, what wilt thou have me to do? . . . Arise, and go to . . . " The wailing of his children and his nephews and nieces are also mixed together when oneofus comes to the stairs and, as he continues to upbraid and castigate himself: "It would be different if you had been downstairs . . . none of these cries would be happening . . . " he carries on asking: "Why are they all crying? . . . what's happened?" As we descend the stairs, staying with oneofus as he hurries down, the wailing of the children turns into a viscous sound that clings to everything and makes everything sorrowful, while the sound of womanwhopreaches grows quieter still, becoming an intermittent murmur: "And the men which . . . stood speechless . . . when his eyes were opened, he saw no man . . . the persecutor was blind . . ." Beside himself with worry, Germán Alcántara Carnero, who now skips across the buckled tiles that serve as the flooring here, rushes headlong down the passageway, and upon hearing the wailing fall quiet, wonders: *Why nothing now . . . why aren't they crying anymore?* at the same time as he asks himself: *Why is his door open . . . why didn't you come down earlier?* Womanwhopreaches' voice is less than a murmur now, just a drip: "They took . . . three . . . not drinking . . . evenings . . . sight . . .", and when the kitchen door comes in sight oneofus thunders: "You should have come down at sunrise! . . . you swore, a family that you would give yourself to . . . you ought to have said: 'read to me later on . . .' or perhaps you believe you should have let her read to you before?"

He enters the kitchen to find the siblings and cousins of bornsickly standing around the inert body. Germán Alcántara Carnero, trembling, drops to the ground. He begins to sob, berating himself: "How many times

did I say: 'listen to her' . . . how many times: 'just pay attention' . . . you should have listened every time she told you: 'it's because of all that you did in the past' . . . "
Lifting his face up, Germán Alcántara Carnero looks at the weeping children and shouts: "What has happened to your brother?" The children look down at the violet floor tiles and again hear ourman: "What are you doing out of your room? What was *he* doing out of his room?"

If you hadn't been upstairs none of this would have happened.

He can still make out his wife's voice, and for a moment he finds it calming, and he sees bornsickly more clearly for a moment: a strange whiteness shadows his mouth. Putting his forefinger and middle fingers into his mouth, Germán Alcántara Carnero pushes his fingers in a little deeper still, beyond his second knuckles, and with a heave succeeds in dislodging half a rabbit skull, which he holds for a moment, staring at it, then smashes on the floor.

His wife's words drift down: "And he was with them, moving about freely in Jerusalem, speaking out boldly in the name of the Lord . . . "

Not stopping to clean his son's saliva from his fingers, Germán Alcántara Carnero rips the trinket from around his own neck, a trinket that he has worn for so many years, and, as clouds eclipse his pupils, holds it out as an offering to bornsickly. The trinket is comprised of the chain that used to be Delsagrado's and of the bullet that one day, in the early hours of November 18, 1944, in the moment shortly to be recounted, penetrated his chest.

When Dolores Enriqueta appears in the kitchen, towing her words behind her like a balloon vendor towing his wares, still she is reciting: "Then had the churches rest throughout all Judaea and Galilee and Samaria, and were edified; and walking in the fear of the Lord, and in the comfort of the Holy Ghost, were multiplied . . . " Ourman lifts his son into his arms and tries to hand him to her but, just as was the case eight years ago, a distorted look enters the woman's face:

"Put him somewhere else, anywhere—I don't intend to carry him."

A couple of seconds elapse, and she begins reading once more: "Israelite born in Tarsus . . . "

The children break down crying again, and as ourman asks himself: *Should you, too, be looking for solace?* our story departs from the place and the moment it was in.

Our story must now depart this October morning and cross twenty-four years, one month, several days, and a few hours, and a stretch of the Mesa Madre Buena itself to arrive at kilometer twenty-one of the track that connects La Cruz to the dam, thereby landing in the bright moment at the end of which ourman will find his ribs, chest, and stomach drenched in blood.

Early morning on November 18, 1944, just before sunrise, the hour when the sierra and cordilleras that rise up on all sides of the Mesa Madre Buena emerge from shadows like whales surfacing from the water, Germán Alcántara Carnero, who six and a quarter hours ago was finally handed the letter he had been waiting to receive—*You decide what to do with those who do not want to join and you should also deal with these men . . . show no mercy to those who do not want to join the movement!*—and who now brings his attention back to the interior of the car we are riding in, says: "Stop by that tree over there!" Juan Ignacio el Negro Romo Hernández, Will D. Glover, Óscar el Chino López Ley, and Ramiro la Madrina López Palas are in the car, too—the same car the ministry was given just a couple of years ago. "There, by the pepper tree!"

When the car we are traveling in—a black 1940 Chevrolet de Luxe—comes to a stop, the silence, a dense and sticky absence of sound, is broken only by the caustic screech of the rubber scraping the window as it is lowered. Resting an arm on the window he has opened, Germán Alcántara Carnero looks off into the distance and sees, through the dust-covered, bug-spattered windscreen, the three floodlights at the entrance to the dam. "Didn't I tell you it was only two hundred meters from this spot?" Before any of the others—who'd said: "I bet it's at least half a kilometer"—can say anything, the three floodlights flicker off for a moment, and then, after another unsettled palpitation, they go out fully—plunging our final destination into darkness. Screwing up his face, turning on the small ceiling light, and turning around to face his men again, El Gringo Alcántara Carnero asks: "Are you sure there isn't anyone at this entrance? No guards at all?"

"That's what Adalberto told me and El Chino," says La Madrina.

"And that's what the guys we got in the night said," says El Chino, elbowing Will and saying: "Right? Didn't they?"

"That's what they said," says Will, "no guards on Thursdays. The floodlights must be there to make people *think* there's guards."

Ourman's face stiffens as he peers out into the darkness. The floodlights flicker once more. "They wouldn't go on and off like that if someone was there doing it . . . they wouldn't be, you know, trembling like that . . . " When he says the word "trembling," Germán Alcántara Carnero realizes his two hands are trembling and, placing them on the dashboard, says to himself: *it must be because I haven't slept*, while out loud issuing a threat: "I hope for all your sakes you're right about the guards . . . " Then, placing the letter inside—the letter given to him nearly seven hours earlier now—he unlocks his door. "Stay here, the lot of you . . . you haven't come to help me today . . . " Taken aback, La Madrina, El Negro, El Chino, and Will watch as El Gringo Alcántara Carnero opens the door, gets out, and walks away, chewing on these words: "You decide what to do . . . do not want to join . . . these men . . . no mercy to those who do not want . . . the movement!"

Walking past the tree he previously indicated, his legs have begun trembling in the same way that the limbs of hunting dogs tremble before a hunt. *This can't be the lack of sleep*, says ourman, glimpsing in the early morning light the stream that runs half a meter deep, large white boulders lining its edge: *I can't let the pain of María get to me today . . . I have to concentrate . . .* Then, out loud: "If I come down between the agaves and those *pulques*, I can get to the stream and from there make it over to those stones." Then, glancing up at the horizon and the light blue-gray strip gradually illuminating the tops of the sierra: *It's getting light already . . . I'm going to get there and they'll all be awake . . . if I don't go down now they'll see me coming . . . and they'll have a chance to get ready.*

The men in the car watch as their boss hurries away.

"What's going on with El Gringo?" asks La Madrina for the third or fourth time this morning: "Since when has he cared about orders? And anyway, why would they have told him to go on his own?"

"There's no way," says Will, unlocking his door, "they told him to go on his own . . . Do you think they would have told him to deal with six men alone?"

Though only Will D. Glover has suddenly understood what's happening, El Negro nods and unlocks his door as well: "Who's gonna be the faggot who stays in the car?"

At the bottom of the slope, where a rocky stretch of ground gives way to weeds and plants, their boss hurries on, all the while murmuring to himself: "You'll forgive me, for though it might seem like a betrayal, it isn't . . . you wouldn't want me to get to the dam with my mind all over the place and then get shot down . . . From here on it's just me and these bastards holed up in the dam . . . nothing's gonna knock me off." But not even ourman is capable of imagining—though in this case it would be better to say "is capable of remembering"—what it is that is truly dragging him off course.

Coming past fig trees and pepper trees, and the tall flowering agaves that rise into the sky like crosses and the cacti brought by the engineers sent from the ministry, up ahead the floodlights are still blinking on and off. *That's the shortest route*, thinks ourman, seeing a path now fifteen meters ahead. *It'll be light any minute . . . get a move on*, he thinks, only to pull up suddenly and turn back; head bowed, he retraces his steps for a distance, murmuring: "If I've stopped thinking about her, why am I still distracted? What's stopping me from concentrating . . . what is happening right now . . . what happened in this place?"

"Why's he left the path?" asks La Madrina, and then: "The dam's the other way!"

"He's going to take the stream," says El Negro, coming forward on all fours. "More cover along the stream . . ."

"We should go after him."

"Wait, he might see us," says El Chino, grabbing El Negro by the ankle: "Once he's in the stream, once he's made it to the rocks, then we'll have some cover, too."

We'll be the last thing on his mind, thinks Will D. Glover, the only one who knows what's really happening, why today ourman has become someone else, why he isn't fully here, why he isn't feeling just angry today, but in fact guilty as well.

"Once he gets to the stream, me and El Chino will head down after him. You two, go get the car and drive round to the far side of the dam, and go the long way round."

El Gringo Alcántara Carnero reaches the edge of the stream, which cuts along half a meter deep, and uses a blasted fig tree to lower himself in. The shock of the icy water stops him for a moment, even as it prompts his four men to set off.

Then, in the early morning quiet, a clattering noise goes up to the right of El Gringo: a barn owl has fallen clumsily to the ground, the branch on which it was perched having suddenly snapped. Ourman stays stock-still, eyes fixed on the dam ahead, inside which the barn owl's fall has awoken a pair of brothers. They fell asleep leaning up against one another, and now strain to hear any further evidence of an attack, though they do not yet know they are under attack. After a few moments' silence they shut their eyes, though sleep eludes them.

They are the commanders of the three or four rebels still left at the dam, which is the way of things in this country when any kind of uprising breaks out: after a few days the rebels go home, annoyed at themselves for having risen up, regretting they've tried to change the situation, and frightened to no longer be obeying—above all horrified at the thought that the world might suddenly be theirs.

The tops of the sierra are now aflame, all the colors of the world's molten armature suddenly on display. Ourman begins wading cautiously ahead, trying not to splash too loudly. As he thinks, *Nothing's happened . . . nothing's stopping me . . . I am the master of this moment . . . no one's stopping me from carrying out my orders*, he also asks himself in a quiet voice, without knowing why or where the question comes from: "Now do you remember what happened up ahead? What happened up at the end of those rocks? Who it was that died in this place, long ago? And right around this time of day?" The answer fails to fully take form, and he hurries on, soon clambering out of the stream and arriving at the end of the natural formation that divides the thicketland and the deep part of the scrubland. Walking numbly ahead, ourman is unable to quiet the last question he put to himself, or to quite govern his two legs, which stride faster and faster on, carrying him ever closer to the dam—the side entrance has now come into view. *Keep your head down after the rocks . . . either cross the open ground keeping low, or just run . . .* And once more, without intending to, he hears himself murmur: "This was where you fell . . . this was where you drew your last breath . . . here, where I am right now . . . " Trembling, transported back to the morning of El Demónico Camilo Mónico Macías Osorio's death, he says: "We came to turf out the old townspeople . . . the families living on the lands flooded by the dam water . . . this was where you drew your last . . . right where I am now . . . " At this, ourman shouts a furious lament, one rooted in a moment four years before, one that now fully awakens the men in the dam, and one that carries back to La Madrina and Will.

"Why the hell's he broken cover . . . " demands La Madrina. "Why's he calling out . . . why's he not keeping to the rocks?"

Will D. Glover grabs his arm, and they both listen:

"I'm talking to the men in the dam . . . " cries El Gringo Alcántara Carnero. "Come out or I'm going to come in there . . . it'd be better for you if you come out right now!"

Hurrying forward, and deciding to raise his voice even louder—convinced that he has no choice in the matter—ourman shouts and shouts, while thinking to himself: *So this was what made me lie to them today . . . tell them that I had orders to come alone . . . I was worried there'd be another accident . . . another of my men might die . . . these idiots, they've followed me—how could they think I wouldn't see them—they really thought I wouldn't notice?* Looking back over his shoulder, El Gringo Alcántara Carnero sees La Madrina and Will keeping low in the water.

He's remembered that morning! thinks Will, he himself remembering El Demónico Macías's death, the day they found that their boss had more to him than rage alone—the day it became apparent there was a place in his soul for guilt and sadness, too.

"Come out this instant!" he cries, turning back to the dam. "Don't tell me you can't hear me. Don't tell me you weren't expecting me!" The guilt, the anger, the powerlessness, and the sadness of the death of El Demónico drop away as he advances on the dam. "Come and see, I'm here on my own . . . no one's with me!" The same guilt, anger, powerlessness, and sadness that on a distant day, twelve years from the morning we are currently witnessing, will prompt him to forsake the ministry—and make him then grasp at anything that might explain why he did so—the bullet in his chest, Anne Lucretius Ford's death, the mere sum of the years, wanting a different life—everything except for the true cause of his departure: the accidental death of El Demónico. It was he who stood beside him during his rise through the ministry ranks, who was with him on his return to the Mesa Madre Buena, and before that, all through the years spent far away from this country, during the war, during the end of his childhood, and in the encounter with the Díaz Cervantes brothers.

"Come out of the dam this instant . . . let's see if you've got the balls!" cries ourman—whom we would do well to

call *manwhotrembles* for now—maddened and gripped by
a memory that until today, November 18, 1944, he had
buried, and which very soon, at 06:29, to be exact, will
be buried again—this time for a full thirty years. Only on
the final afternoon of his life will this memory emerge out
of the depths from which it steers the rest of his life, and
that will also be the time to speak of El Demónico Macías
and of the accidents that led to his demise on these very
rocks now echoing ourman's words: " . . . the balls to take
me on . . . I'm not leaving until you come out . . . at least
let me see your faces . . . can't you see it's your lucky day!"

Unbeknownst to him the two rebel leaders, the Díaz
Cervantes brothers, Baldomero and Macario, are looking
down at him from one of the windows. The same men
who nearly thirty years ago, along with their three now
deceased brothers, took ourman in.

"He's come alone," says Macario, ducking down from
the window.

"Didn't I tell you he'd come looking for us?" says
Baldomero, before ordering the others: "No one move.
Hold your positions."

Ourman spreads his arms and throws back his head—
while inside the dam the Díaz Cervantes brothers unbolt

the door. All the memories have passed through him now, and he bellows in fury: "Do you not see, you'll never get lucky like this again . . . I don't mean to put up a fight!" while he thinks: *All the better that it should be the Díaz Cervantes boys!* and smiles as he remembers gripping Demetrio's throat in his hands, the man's stifled entreaties, his throbbing face, the tears and the excitement and preoccupation that crossed El Demónico's face, who stood two meters off saying: "Let him go before they get here . . . we need to get out of here right now!" "What are you waiting for? Want me to toss my gun? Fine!" shouts ourman, flinging away his weapon, spreading his arms again.

La Madrina, running along the stream, calls back over his shoulder at Will D. Glover: "He's totally lost it."

"You cover his left side," Will shouts, jumping up and coming past La Madrina, adding as he sees the dam entrance swing open: "Get down, and get your piece out . . . they're opening that gate." By the time Baldomero and Macario hear Will's voice and the ensuing sound of his gunshots, they have already opened the gate and all that remains is to return fire and hide. Bullets fly, and ourman hits the ground, tumbling back into the stream.

It is 06:29 on November 18, 1944, and the moment we were in has come to an end.

Bullets continue to fly as the blood from ourman's sternum in the water imitates the motion of a streamer blown on by a young boy with all his might. The shots and the shouting will last a few more minutes, and then El Negro and El Chino will suddenly arrive at the dam and ambush the rebels, who, half an hour later, tied to huge rocks, will be drowned in the stagnant dam water, according to the order ourman would have given had he not been unconscious. But this doesn't concern us now. Germán Alcántara Carnero faints, still floating in the stream, while his mind goes back to the day he returned to the Mesa Madre Buena with El Demónico Macías at his side, and to the afternoon he became the leader of the ministry.

THE ASCENTS

THIS STORY HAS NOW ARRIVED at the moments recalled by Germán Alcántara Carnero as he lay wounded twenty meters away from the dam: his return to the Mesa Madre Buena, and his rise through the ranks of the small ministry he would later go on to lead. As well as illuminating the length and breadth of ourman's life, these two moments light up the existence of two other human beings: Anne Lucretius Ford and El Demónico Camilo Mónico Macías Osorio—the threads of whose lives at some point became entangled with those of ourman, forming a knot this story must unravel.

At 13:02 on February 17, 1934, five years, ten months, and eleven days after the morning when ourman came back to the Mesa with El Demónico and Will D. Glover—a return journey that will be dissected at the end of the day in which we now find ourselves—Germán Alcántara Carnero looks down at his wounded shoulder as innumerable dry leaves dance and twirl in the distance, and as, farther off in the ravine between the mountains, a column of black smoke twists skyward—a serpent devouring a church. El Gringo Alcántara Carnero squints, as do the pair of men beside him—a pair that would be a trio if Ignacio del Sagrado Sandoval-Íñiguez Martínez and his men hadn't killed ourman's boss, Teobaldo Pascua Gómez.

"No one's coming after us now . . . not one of them," he says. "Didn't I tell you they wouldn't have the balls to come through the scrublands?"

"*He* said that?" says El Demónico, elbowing Will D. Glover and saying: "I was the one who said they wouldn't come down after us . . . they don't like it out on open ground."

"What does it matter now who said it?" says Will, shading his eyes and swiveling around. "We made it, that's what matters." The wind picks up at their backs as they set off again.

"What was that noise?" asks El Demónico. "Is that someone shouting?"

"That was no shout . . . " cries ourman over the whistling wind—a gale that began to blow an hour ago, buffeting them with dust and stones. Gripping his bleeding shoulder, he turns to Will D. Glover: "How do you suppose we break it to him that Teobaldo's dead . . . and that we left his body up there?"

"Telling Don Dante is the least of our problems . . . " Will D. Glover says, glancing nervously at ourman's shoulder. "How the hell do we break it to the twins that their dad's dead?"

The wind at their backs, the three men stumble on, each picturing the moment when Teobaldo hit the ground. They had instantly begun arguing: "We can't carry him with us . . . especially not without any horses . . . " "*You* want to carry him? With your shoulder like that! None of us'll make it back alive." The wind drops for a moment, and the shrieking sound can be heard once more.

"There it is again!" says El Demónico Macías, stopping dead: "Don't tell me you didn't hear it this time," he says, grabbing Will D. Glover and El Gringo Alcántara Carnero, who says at the top of his voice:

"I heard it . . . I heard a shout."

"No," says Will, brushing El Demónico's fingers from his elbow. "That was something barking." He points toward a number of moving smudges in the distance, seen for a moment and then obscured by the whirls of eddying dust. The whipping wind pelts them with loose stones, dry leaves, and scraps of wood.

Leaning close together, they form a tight triangle and shield their faces, shouting over the wind: "How do we tell them they killed Teobaldo?" "Who wants to be the one to say we left the boss's body up there?" To say that they fear the reaction of Manuel Dante Creel Otero is putting it mildly: the man who reigns over this mesa terrifies ourmen, whom we will only refer to as *ourmen* in this paragraph, given that this is the single moment in which the trio's fears are so aligned—fears they face up to by trying to avoid them, each escaping into thoughts of his own past. Thoughts, in the case of Germán Alcántara Carnero, of the dogs he once owned; of childhood sandstorms and devastation in the case of El Demónico Macías; and in Will D. Glover's, thoughts of the accursed day when he said: "Let me come with you"—all moments we will return to.

The three men, briefly and quite mistakenly feeling hopeful that the lull in the wind means it's died down for good, know very well that they don't have any choice but to go and speak with Don Dante, and yet they continue to drag their feet, carried forward by a kind of inertia, a vague and obscure pulse in their bodies as they draw closer to the home of a man none of them has set eyes on before, though his name is spoken among them most days.

"Might it be his dogs?" El Demónico asks as they pass the animals, a group circling around a bitch in heat, barking and drooling.

"What would Don Dante want with so many dogs?" he says, though only to stave off the thought: *What is Don Dante going to do with us?* Reaching across and squeezing his shoulder hard—the pain is a stimulus and just about the only thing keeping his heavy eyelids from dropping—El Gringo Alcántara Carnero musters what strength remains him. And now, as he urges his colleagues on, we will do better to refer to him as *manwhoascends*, at least until this part of the story is complete, a story that has by now crossed its middle point. "All that matters is getting to his house . . . whatever happens after that, happens . . . we *couldn't* stop for the body . . . Don Dante would hardly have been happy if none of us had come back—if none of us had lived to tell him what happened!"

El Demónico and Will turn ourman's words over in their thoughts, and Teobaldo's final order comes to them once more:

"Get down to the ravine!" he had cried as Delsagrado's men appeared, guns blazing. "Whatever happens, one of us has to get back!"

Will murmurs, half to himself: "We were told they'd all be inside the church . . . How were we supposed to know Delsagrado wasn't in there . . . that he'd seen the fire and brought men?"

For a couple of minutes, the three men we are following trudge on in silence, chewing on Teobaldo's words: *At least one of us has to get away . . . Don't go along the trail, the ravine is better . . . Whatever happens, one of us has to get back . . . Don Dante's expecting us back.*

"There's the house!" El Demónico suddenly cries, breaking the silence, and silencing the memory of Teobaldo. In the distance, beyond a line of cypresses and pepper trees and a gully with a stream at the bottom—a stream that will one day feed a large dam—stands the home of Manuel Dante Creel Otero, the former owner and the current master of this vast mesa. He has recently become a government minister, thereby exchanging the tangible ownership of his kingdom for an intangible, and yet superior form of ownership.

When they are thirty meters short of the house where Don Manuel Dante Creel Otero lives with his wife and three daughters, ourman sees a curtain move, and a figure at the window disappear—the same window through which, many years later, Germán Camilo Alcántara Celis's face will look out.

Don Dante appears when they reach the doorstep:

"Where's Teobaldo?"

They glance at one another, but say nothing. Don Dante gives a pensive nod and motions them through into the living room. He points them to their seats, and after looking his guests over—each with eyes fixed on the floor—commands:

"Out with it now."

"They came out of nowhere!" "We'd burned the church!" "Ten or eleven of them, plus Delsagrado!" "Wasn't inside the church!" "We had it on good information!"

Leaning back in the chair he has elected to sit in, Don Dante waves a hand to quiet the dust-covered young men. After a moment, manwhoascends goes on:

"We ran back to the horses, but they'd slit their throats."

"And Teobaldo?"

"He was shouting at us to leave the horses, to take the ravine way down, and it was just then . . . Then a bullet went clean through his head."

Don Dante has been racking his brains trying to recall where he knows ourman from, and at the mention of Teobaldo's death, with the image of a gunshot to the head, the memory is dislodged . . . *It's him! The boy who stuck his fingers in the dead man's skull and smelled the blood!*

"You're that boy," Don Dante suddenly says. "The day before the uprising began . . . the morning before everything changed." A gust of wind hits the front door, blowing it open and knocking over a low table. Without a word, Don Dante gets up, shuts the door, and, looking incredulously at manwhoascends, comes back to his chair: "I said to myself that day: don't forget this boy . . . Something told me you'd show up again one day . . . You shoved your finger in the bullet wound that day and *smelled* it . . . then you said something like, 'that's what you get'?"

Manwhoascends smiles: "Yes, I told him that's what he got for hurting my beetle. He'd taken his machete to this beetle that was going to be a gift." At this, he winces at a jolt of pain from his shoulder.

"Tell you what," says Don Manuel Dante Creel Otero, jumping to his feet, "if that bullet doesn't end up killing you, I'm going to make you the new boss." His face lights up. "How does that sound?"

The three men look confused, none more so than man-whoascends.

"Don't you want to hear the rest?"

"No, I don't care," says Don Dante, pointing to the door: "What you need to do is get back to the ministry, it shouldn't be left unmanned for so long . . . Don't worry about Teobaldo, I'll send somebody for his body."

Going over to the door, Don Dante holds out a set of keys to ourman and indicates an imported Count Trossi SSK parked a little way from the house: "We'll talk properly tomorrow . . . today I need to talk to Teobaldo's girls . . . and I'm going to tell them they can work for you."

Nodding and turning toward the car, ourman takes his two colleagues by the elbows and, once they are out of earshot, says, "Right, forget about Teobaldo now, and get me to the chemist . . . I can't take this pain anymore."

Once they are in the car, El Demónico at the wheel and manwhoascends in the passenger seat, Will reaches forward and applies pressure to the shoulder wound. Manwhoascends, hand dropping to his lap, is moments from passing out, as his thoughts travel back to Will offering to come with him, to accompany him on his flight back to this country. Will, hand covered in blood, pictures the very same scene: "I need to come with you . . . " he said. "I want to leave and never come back . . . and besides, you'll never find your way without me! I'm not going back down there!" Will begged his foreign friends, pointing to the entrance of the mine they had been working in together, a mine they would have carried on at had El Gringo Alcántara Carnero not grown fond of the local stray dogs, and had some of the local men not started using the dogs for sport.

"Go on then, get your things. We're going in an hour, before they find the bodies and put two and two together, and before one of them tells someone about the fight."

Happy at this acceptance, happy, that is, to be leaving behind his life at the mine, Will D. Glover went and gathered all his earthly belongings: a piece of a mirror, a slightly warped shaving razor, a rope and an iron pick, and set off with his two foreign friends. He did not know—none of them knew—that fate was yet to add another person to their band of fugitives, and lead them back to the country ourman claimed to have left behind. So, at 14:22 on April 6, 1928, five years, ten months, eleven days, and nearly twenty-three hours before the moment when ourman is appointed head of the ministry—at the hour of the day when people are inside their homes, putting food inside themselves, sleeping—Germán Alcántara Carnero, El Demónico Camilo Mónico Macías Osorio, Will D. Glover, and Anne Lucretius Ford cross the town square of Lago Seco. The journey that brought them here was long and difficult: 2,170 kilometers covered in six weeks, 730 of which they spent hidden on three different trains, 831 of which they rode in a stolen car, a Rolls-Royce Tiger Car they abandoned at the border, and 609 of which they walked. After splashing their faces and taking long drinks at the fountain, the woman and the three men set out walking once more and come onto Calle Candelaria, where they look around in surprise at the empty streets: the mill, the barbershop, and the button shop are yet to open, nor have the locks come off at the dentist or the cheese shop that was once a poulterer's before the swollen kidney epidemic and the decimation of the avian population on the Mesa Madre Buena.

"We leave town on the north side, go all the way along that end," says El Gringo Alcántara Carnero, pointing: "then we take a path out beyond the cemetery. Then it's straight on to a hacienda, take another path and go to a rocky area, then through some thicketland . . . keeping these enormous white rocks always in sight . . . damn if I don't remember those white rocks . . . get to them and you're nearly at my home . . . " And upon saying these words, "my home," Germán Alcántara Carnero feels a chill, and wonders: *Might anyone still be living there? Might Heredí and Mother still be there? Or just my sister on her own?* Ourman shakes his head, driving away such thoughts: *You'll find out when you get there.*

Reaching the corner of Calle Independencia and Distrito, Anne Lucretius Ford calls out: "Unless you get us lost again."

"What did I *say* about her coming along?" says El Demónico Macías. "How many times did I tell you? She isn't ever going to shut that mouth of hers. Get a good fistful of earth in there and it still won't do no good."

"What about him," says Will D. Glover. "He's hardly the quietest guy around . . . he's the one who never knows when to shut up!"

"Listen," says ourman, cutting them off: "We knew it wasn't going to be easy, but we're very nearly there now. Why don't we *all* shut up for a bit? How about we all agree to say nothing till we get to my house—how about that?"

The same shudder stops ourman in his tracks as they come past the ministry building where he will one day rule, and where, later, finding himself utterly exhausted, he will say to himself: *I'm leaving today, forever.*

He knows nothing about any of that, however. His thoughts are of his childhood home: *What will I do if the two of them are living there? What if Heredí has started her own family there? Or if some other bastards have set up shop there?*

A couple of blocks farther on, coming onto Yotepec de Covarrubias, El Gringo Alcántara Carnero, who has tried to stop imagining his mother and sister, and his fictive nephew and brothers-in-law, looks up and, pointing at the misty horizon, adds: "Those arches up there are part of the cemetery. We need to go around the cemetery to get out onto the scrubland."

The sensation of finally arriving, which makes their feet feel less heavy, also has the effect of sending their minds back through the journey and the events that forced them to set out in the first place—as though the sensation of arrival somehow frees them to begin accounting for all that has passed. Anne Lucretius's thoughts turn to her parents and her brother; Will thinks of the days he spent down the mine and, not for the first time, praises the day he convinced the others to let him come along; while El Demónico thinks of the work he and ourman also took on a cotton plantation, and gives thanks it's all over.

The man who is ourman, beset not just by thoughts of the past but by future intimations as well, shakes his head and comes back into the present moment as they leave the cemetery behind, the huge expanse of the mesa unfolding before them.

He stops for a moment and casts around:

"This way," he says, starting forward again. "Over to those rocks . . . the path comes after that."

And as he picks his way down the steep slope his mind is filled with people that are not real: *What will I do if Heredí and Mother are there? Or if there are strangers in my home? Or . . . if she didn't die that day? And if my father didn't die? If nothing actually happened to my María?*

While Germán Alcántara Carnero, floundering in fear and remembering his father's gaze—the one eye diurnal and the other nocturnal—begins along the path they have been aiming for, finding himself on land worked by him and by his father before—the others continue to think about the recent days: Anne about the afternoon she left her home and went away with ourman, a man she knew close to nothing about, thereby choosing to love one of her father's workers and not her God, her siblings, or her history. She had run to the redwoods where Will, ourman, and El Demónico were waiting. Anne Lucretius says to herself: *Now we'll find out if it was worth it.*

El Demónico and Germán Alcántara Carnero—the latter, turning at the first fork in the path, tries to banish people he thought dead from his mind—had already decided to leave the mine when they found themselves ambushed by Will D. Glover, who is currently bringing up the rear as they pass siding stands that ourman and his father worked a long time ago, back when this decaying hacienda wasn't just this pile of masonry and black stone—stone and masonry that ourman will later use to build a new family home, the birthplace of bornsickly, and the place where ourman will eventually die—on a day that awaits us in the next chapter. "I have to come with you . . . I want to leave and never come back . . . let me come with you!" El Demónico remembers Will saying. "Not a bad idea . . . and maybe he could help guide us . . . " ourman had said. "Think this foreigner can be trusted?" "Yes, I think we can trust the little miner man . . . " "Shall we tell him it's a yes, then?"

With Will as their guide, they traversed forests and mountains and came to a town where they took a passenger train. When the sun came up the next day, they looked out the window and saw large numbers of black slaves working the land. They met the owner of an enormous plantation—he, having lost his white workers nine days when his son took against them, contracted ourman, Will, and El Demónico—who now skips forward three weeks in his thoughts, recalling the morning when Germán Alcántara Carnero came running into the eating area and shouted in his ear:

"I slept with Ana!"

"She isn't called Ana, you idiot," said El Demónico: "Her name's Anne. Anyway, what the fuck were you thinking? Didn't I tell you to steer clear of that girl?"

The quartet have come to the barrenest portion of the vast swath of thickets and scrub, and ourman's thoughts of their destination have become frenzied: *What will I do if he's there waiting for me? If Father has waited all these years for me to get back . . . if I have to face him again today . . . this time it won't be a stone I'll use . . . I won't use anything . . . I'll just use these two hands . . . what does it matter if María's there . . . if he didn't actually do anything to her . . . he'd already done plenty.*

"Idiot, you're going to get us thrown out . . . that's if he doesn't kill us first!"

"How are they going to throw us out if they don't even know about it?"

"Don't you get it? He's sure to find out . . . For all we know he already suspects, and he's her father, he's doubtless got ways of making her talk!"

At this point Will D. Glover had interrupted: "We're going to have to hit the road again . . . " He and El Demónico had looked at each other, before saying, almost in unison:

"We won't have a choice . . . if he finds out, he'll kill us!"

Now, Will overtakes Anne Lucretius Ford on her left-hand side, so that she is bringing up the rear as they approach the midway point of the rocky outcrop, the place in which we earlier saw three dogs devour an opossum family. Will gains on ourman, whose pace momentarily slows—weighed down by the great number of hypothetical people in his mind, and by a rapid series of answers to his own questions:

If I have to take him on again, I'll use these two hands and nothing else . . . what does it matter if María's there . . . he did plenty already . . . what will I do then with María . . . I won't hurt María . . . or maybe I'll have to . . . I'll have to hurt her, too . . . but I don't want to hurt her!

It was Will who had seen the dogs being starved, beaten, and made to fight at the mine—dogs that El Gringo Alcántara Carnero had been taking care of, and had been going around for a number of days asking after. Will had seen the ring the men set up, had witnessed the arrival of the thirty or so individuals who had come to bet on the dogs, had witnessed the spectacle until, as people had started to leave, ourman had appeared: without a single word to anyone he had grabbed a pick and struck down the two organizers of the evening. Will knew this meant that El Demónico and Germán Alcántara Carnero—who, as they get to the end of the rocky outcrop where the slate shines like shards of glass, is still struggling in his mind against his sister's fate—would have to leave, and he had gone and begged them to bring him along. And four days after the day that Will is replaying as he, quickening his pace, draws level with ourman, the three men who at the beginning of this chapter we called ourmen had found work at the cotton plantation that El Demónico is now revisiting in his thoughts, and where Anne Lucretius Ford was born twenty years ago and where ourman fell in love for the first time. As Will draws level with ourman, the latter announces:

"Leave me alone, I've got a lot on my mind . . . Why don't you get the others to hurry up . . . we're practically there now!"

Will obediently drops back, while El Gringo Alcántara Carnero, without breaking stride, picks up a rock from the path:

"Just this hill and then down the other side!"

Falling quiet again and breaking into a run, Germán Alcántara Carnero wonders: *What do I say if there are other shacks there now, or other people? Or if my shack isn't empty . . . if it isn't empty, my home?* As he thinks these last two words, "my home," ourman accelerates once more and, driven on by a strange inexplicable force, reaches the brow of the hill—passing three agaves, four yuccas, a pair of pepper trees, ten bishop's weeds, and the fig tree—he reaches the top just as we prepare to depart from this current moment, arriving at the summit of the hill that looks out over a landscape he has looked out over and has cast his mind back to so many times and that now, for the first time in his life, does not leave him crestfallen. At the foot of the hill, the ground for several hundred meters is a black stain, an enormous ash-black stain, at the center of which lies a ruined shack, dilapidated and dust-covered, the same dust that at the very end of this story will inter both the body of ourman and his memory. Next to the broken-down shack, and just as we are in the process of departing from this moment, we see the corpse of what looks like some large animal, and the only thing in the vicinity that seems to have escaped the flames unscathed: it is the fig tree that was formerly used to hang up the clothes of the family whose son we now leave as he descends the hillside—passing the three crosses that stand like fearful unsteady stalks and that fill the approaching figure with the hope that had drained out of him almost two hours ago—in the moment when he said to himself, for the first time today and for the first time in this life: my home.

EXEQUIES

THIS STORY'S LAST CHAPTER—a story that via the fluctuations in one man's life renders the fluctuations of an era and of the place always known to its inhabitants as the Mesa Madre Buena—dissects the final two moments to shed light on the life of Germán Alcántara Carnero. These two moments, unlike the others we have dissected—the birth of ourman, his struggles against his father, the disappearance of his younger sister, the fight with the Díaz Cervantes clan, the departure to another kingdom, the conflicts in the borderlands, his return to this mesa, Anne Lucretius Ford's death in an ambush, the burning down of the church on the mountainside, his rise to become chief of the small ministry in Lago Seco, the accident that led to the death of El Demónico

Macías, the torture of the men inside the old slaughter-house, the vengeance taken on Delsagrado as an old man, a self-inflicted punishment before the gates to a dam, the renunciation of the ministry and of a way of life, the meeting with Dolores Enriqueta Celis Gómez, the founding of his family, the birth of an oldest son and that son's ill-health and untimely death—occupy the same amount of time in the life of ourman as they do in this story about him.

And a story may have no beginning, it may even have numerous beginnings, or follow one thread or skip from moment to moment, but it may not end just anywhere: a story's end must match the end of the life that animated it. It is a story I pointlessly tried to insert myself into, forcing me to ask why I wanted to be part of the story to begin with: *Because my days are empty,* I say, *because I am really no different from my contemporaries, because I'm determined to create an imaginary life while my own life unravels in this time of vacuity and pointlessness, because I'm content with being merely the context and never the text itself.* A story that is about to turn to the moments after the unintended death of his son bornsickly: his final attempt to gain mastery over his fate. Two moments that run in sequence and begin here:

At 03:32 on February 18, 1975, when the moon positions itself at the center of the night and owls traverse the skies, Germán Alcántara Carnero opens his eyes wide in fright, seeing before him the nightmare from which he has just awoken: a woman shut inside the trunk, crying out for somebody to help her—a woman who is an amalgam of Anne Lucretius Ford, María del Sagrado Alcántara Carnero, and Dolores Enriqueta Celis Gómez.

Burying his face in his massive hands, ourman groans, begging for this dream image to go away, though he knows—too well—how much he deserves it, this punishment, being visited by the sight of all the women he has ever loved shut inside the same trunk he employed during his time at the ministry. *How many more years of this . . . how long will you have to carry on paying?* ourman asks, massaging his eyeballs, before suddenly crying out "It's the least I deserve: I deserve it all! . . . Do you really think you deserve it? Really, haven't you had enough already?"

"No, not even close," ourman says, peering into the darkness, trying to pick out any detail that might be a way out of this moment: the chair with yesterday's clothes draped over it, a rocking chair his wife gave him as a gift, her Virgin Mary, his charred Christ, the stuffed armadillo

El Trompo Trápaga Mora gave him, the radio that nobody has switched on in years. Reaching down the side of the bed, El Gringo Alcántara Carnero turns on the lamp, and now we see how his face, which rather than seeming to have grown older, simply looks more full of strain and tension. Though it is now six years since he committed himself to the same religion his wife professed silently the moment they met, under her breath when they moved into this house, out loud after giving birth to bornsickly, and at the top of her voice following the death of that child, Germán Alcántara Carnero has found the way to neither forgiveness nor solace.

"You really believe you haven't had enough . . . that this is the way to find forgiveness and solace . . . and all that's happened hasn't been because of something else . . . Really think you couldn't have got it all wrong?" ourman asks himself again while casting around, and then looking down, astonished, at his wife, saying: "Truly, I don't think it has been enough . . . I will find forgiveness one day, but not today . . . this is a trial I have to pass . . . this is the final stage before solace is mine!" Still watching Dolores Enriqueta's cold face, half-lit by the lamp, half in shadow—the same shadows enveloping the rest of this room—Germán Alcántara Carnero thinks on the image he saw in his dream but this time, instead of a chest he sees all the women he has loved in his life shut inside an old casket, so old it looks liable to disintegrate at any moment. He shakes his head and says: "You are my final test . . . I am going to have to get up again . . . to get to my feet even after having been dealt this same blow once again . . . this final step is my way to solace—the solace I didn't find when María died . . . or when Anne or El Demónico died . . . I didn't find it after our son died, either . . . perhaps I will, now that you are dead."

Opening his eyes wide, as though in shock, ourman turns back to the cold and stony countenance beside him, the woman who departed this earth eleven hours ago, a faint red line around her neck from the noose. *What do I tell the children . . . how will I tell them you couldn't stand it any longer . . . that you hanged yourself with the birth ribbon, the one that was meant to bring the child so much luck . . . that the last thing you did was to betray your faith?* Germán Alcántara Carnero asks himself, even as another question takes shape in the recesses of his mind: "Do you really believe this is the way to solace? Maybe she's shown, by betraying you like this, that you got it all wrong? Perhaps you've never had as much faith as you made out . . . Really believe this is the way . . . that solace still might be yours, even now she's done this?" He reaches out to touch the mottled bruises on Dolores Enriqueta's neck, and after a moment, skimming his fingers over the skin, touching it lightly, he suddenly grips her in his hand and begin squeezing, crushing, throttling.

What separates life from death? he thinks, even as he continues to throttle his deceased wife. Strange, in a way, that in the life of ourman—responsible for ending the lives of so many men and women—death, or his fear that his loved ones might die while his love for them is still alive, should be the thing to fuel its most unpredictable turn of events.

"Why did you . . . how is it that . . . what . . . You killed yourself!" Germán Alcántara Carnero then bursts, letting go of Dolores Enriqueta's neck. The moment he opens his eyes, tears begin streaming down his face, thick, salty, almost cloudy-looking tears, and for some minutes he becomes lost in the same feelings, the same corrosive dejection, that engulfed him yesterday when he came in to find his wife dangling from the beams. Before cutting her down, trembling violently and murmuring and weeping, he decided to lie her down in the bed, to spend another night at her side. Maybe in the morning he would know what to do.

And now it is morning. He turns over and sees the curtain move a little, but no, it isn't moving: the hints of early sunlight, and where they meet the darkness of the room, have merely given an impression of movement. Once more he thinks of the frontier between death and life, and again of the pain that always attends deaths, that attended the deaths of María del Sagrado Alcántara Carnero—when he left home—and Anne Lucretius Ford and El Demónico Macías Osorio—when he denounced his work and decided to make a family— and the death of his oldest son—when he committed himself to a faith he had previously spent his life persecuting. He looks over at the chair in which she used to sit reading to him from the book now lying on the floor—the book we saw Dolores Enriqueta Celis Gómez reading from almost six years ago: *And it came to pass,* ourman hears her saying, *that, as I made my journey, and was come nigh unto Damascus about noon, suddenly there shone from heaven a great light round about me. So great was Saul's astonishment . . . Saul, Saul, why persecutest thou me? And I answered, Who are you, Lord? And He said unto me, I am the one you persecute . . .*

This was the passage closest to her heart. He shakes his head and falls back onto the mattress. *Because of you, He won't love me like a son . . . although if He were real He wouldn't have let you . . .* Sitting up, Germán Alcántara Carnero steps off the bed and, regarding the body of the woman we met in the town square of Lago Seco almost twenty years ago, he is confronted with every person whose deaths have touched his life, a cascade of images finally coming to a stop with that of El Demónico Macías. *No*, he thinks, *now is not the time to think about how you died . . . or the existence of God, for fuck's sake . . . just work out what to do with this body. That is all.*

What follows: Germán Alcántara Carnero turning on the remaining lights, going into Dolores Enriqueta's dressing room and hunting through her hundreds of dresses until he finds her favorite—all the while questioning his faith as never before. *If you don't believe in Him, does that also mean not believing in His word?* Going back into the bedroom, he lifts the feather-light body of Dolores Enriqueta into his arms and, slowly and carefully—lovingly, in truth—begins undressing her. He covers her neck with a shawl before sitting down on the bed again, doubting, doubting a God that it is perhaps time to put aside. Once more the cloudy tears come forth. And whatever he does next—pacing the room, drawing the curtains, slowly and agonizingly inching closer to an exit—we will not be privy to, for instead we are on our way to another moment, the moment of El Demónico Macías's death, the same moment ourman hurries off to in his mind in order to avoid both his doubts and the moments that must surely come next.

Though I have no place in this story, though I have to accept that I only want to appropriate this life because my own is such a shit life, though I ought to admit that my existence as a writer is empty and that I only tried to become a character because I have never dared to be a person, I also know about keeping promises, and that is why I take this moment, while ourman absents himself, to recount here the death of El Demónico Macías, a necessary component in this story and a moment when the air is full of dust motes, the sunlight merciless, birds shriek in the distance and circle over the white rocks we saw two chapters ago when ourman called out the rebels at the dam, and Germán Alcántara Carnero, Will D. Glover, and

Amparo Pascua de Ramones are hiding out—Amparo's twin, Ausencia, is lying down on the riverside, her legs in the water, her paint-splattered clothes torn to shreds and her head peeking out between two rocks. Two hours ago, ourman and the twins sent a note to El Demónico, whose thirty-fifth birthday it is today, in which Ausencia said to him: *My love, I'll wait for you today down by the river so we can be together, alone, I don't want to be with the others, I want it to be just me and you and for us to love each other like you love me when I let you. I'm going to let you today, your birthday. My love, meet me at the river at noon, down by the rocks where no one ever goes and where the water is calm and cool. My love, I can't wait to see you . . . I'm so happy you were born.*

A note that sent shudders through him, that nearly made him faint, El Demónico hurried out of the ministry over which ourman has ruled for a little more than two years. He knows very well, as do Germán Alcántara Carnero and Will D. Glover, that the area in which his girlfriend waits is one of the areas controlled by Ignacio del Sagrado Sandoval-Íñiguez Martínez and his men: what he doesn't know, as he runs outside, heart in mouth, is that it is all a trick, a ruse being sprung by his girlfriend and friends. Putting his foot down in the Count Trossi SSK—strangely, it was parked right outside the door—El Demónico Macías crosses Lago Seco—putting his foot down until the vehicle almost takes off—and out onto the surrounding mesa, crossing the expanses of farmland, much of the scrubland, the rocky outcrop, and entering the belt of thicketland where ourman was born, coming to the hill where we spent the beginning of chapter seven's final moment, this craggy hill being as far as the car can go. He has to get out and run, tripping several times as he comes down the hillside in a frenzy, down to the cacti, the yuccas and the tall prickly pears, along the stream bed and then threading his way between the boulders, and is still running when the enormous white rocks that are his destination rear up in the distance.

Hidden behind these white rocks, ourman, Will, and Amparo watch as he approaches, and cannot stop themselves from laughing at the man's anguish as he runs headlong, coming up onto the small promontory where Ausencia lays hidden from sight. When he does see her, on the floor, unmoving, her clothes torn and stained with what he believes to be blood, El Demónico Macías stops, drops to the ground and opens his mouth to cry out, but the only noise to come from his body is the crash and tumble of his pounding heart. Hidden in their cave, his colleagues are still beside themselves, and they talk in low voices while Ausencia, still on the floor—they told her: "Don't get up till you hear us call to you!"—does not know her man has arrived. El Demónico tries to stand, and eventually manages to do so, but after just one step drops to his knees again. It is then, seeing him fall down this second time, that ourman feels bad—he knows what his friend is like—but before he can make it to the cave mouth, and before Ausencia can shout out for him to stop, El Demónico Macías is raising his gun, placing its black barrel in his mouth, and has pulled the trigger. A plume of blood and bone and brain and skull.

"Then the shouting began, the recriminations," says ourman at the top of his voice, as he once more experiences the pain, the guilt, and the terrible depression that inundated his mind at the time. "Then all the shouting, all the recriminations!" El Gringo Alcántara Carnero says, and again once or twice, each time a little more quietly, and he, and we, are back in this present moment:

At 15:56 on February 18, 1975, Germán Alcántara Carnero draws the last of the curtains in his bedroom and looks out into the night—in the silver moonlight the land has the aspect of both metal and velvet. He whispers to himself: "Then all the shouting, all the recriminations . . . same as it was with María and with our son . . . whereas with you, and with Anne, everything just fell silent . . . the silence He demands . . . the silence that might be my way to solace!" While we were away recounting the circumstances of El Demónico's death, ourman picked up the book his wife used to read, and found she had marked a page, and that, before she hanged herself, she had highlighted a certain line:

And immediately there fell from his eyes as it had been scales: and he received sight forthwith, and arose, and was baptized . . .

"The way forward," he whispers, "is not to renounce my faith . . . but rather to allow that faith to deepen!"

He placed the book next to the radio and came and stood by the window, with its view out over the land, the layer of fine-spun metal-velvet covering the land. The lamplight illuminates the garden, in which the children have been playing for some time now: they have continued to inhabit the floor below. *When was the last time they asked after you*, ourman wonders, *the last time one of them came up to see how you were . . . that one of them even spoke your name . . .* Turning to look at Dolores Enriqueta, he says: "How do I make Him forgive you . . . how do I bury you so that He might forgive you . . . how do I go about tricking Him . . . I'm going to need to do something else about your neck . . . I definitely can't tell anyone what's happened!"

The light spilling past him draws the attention of his two dogs, dogs he bought after the death of his oldest son, which then clamber over the ruins of a limewashed wall and come trotting toward the front door.

"Do I bury you in the clothes you chose, or put you in something else . . . put lipstick on you and tie up your hair . . . maybe I use the same bit of ribbon you used to hang yourself!"

Approaching the bed once more, his whole body trembling, ourman points at his wife:

"Maybe you don't deserve to be put in the earth . . . maybe I shouldn't even bury you . . . Maybe I just leave you shut up in here . . . you'll rot in this room if that's what I decide!" While at the same time he says to himself: *What my path needs now is silence . . . my path demands that I be on my own . . . The word of the Lord means I can't have any connection with the world anymore . . . first of all those kids are going to have to go . . . they have to be gone from this house before the day is out.*

It is 04:22 in the morning when he comes down the stairs shouting: "Alonso . . . Enriqueta . . . Mariangeles . . . Ramiro . . . José Julio!"

What follows when ourman comes down the stairs in his house: him entering, one by one, the rooms on the floor where he will spend the rest of his days, him pulling his children and nephews and nieces from their beds and running them out of the house, him falling to his knees on the tiles in the entranceway, just as El Demónico Macías fell to his on the riverside forty-four years and six months ago, and then drawing one of the dogs close and calling after the departed children: "And don't come back . . . Don't come anywhere near this house . . . I don't want you or anyone coming anywhere near this house!"—we are not going to witness because this is the end of this moment, the moment that shows why Germán Alcántara Carnero went on to shun the company of men, and that leads to the final moment in our story, which begins directly:

At 10:08 on November 17, 1981, at the hour, that is, when the birds fly across the Mesa Madre Buena and the dogs lie down for their second siesta of the day, Germán Alcántara Carnero gets up from the armchair he has sat in to read during the last five years and then, going out of the room that one day belonged to bornsickly, says: "What has been, will be." In the hallway, the scene of his children's and his nephews' and nieces' ejection, where he told them never to come back, El Gringo Alcántara Carnero weaves past a half-drunk glass of water, three dog shits, and a yellow plastic bottle and throws the book he inherited from his wife onto a table, raising a cloud of dust when it strikes the top. Stale seclusion hangs heavy on the air.

Crossing the room in which he sleeps and eats and plays with the dogs, Germán Alcántara Carnero, whom we might also call *manwhoregrets*, repeats the phrase: "What has been, will be!" while inwardly saying to himself: *How was I to know that solitary life wasn't the way . . . that the problem wasn't other people . . . that it was no bad thing, in fact, to be connected to the world? It really was simply a question of finding connections with other men.* Stopping at the front door, with the six dogs whining behind him, about to lay his hand on the worm-eaten door handle, he stops, shaken for a moment: it's come again, it's happened to

him again, having to depart a place once more. Reaching
out his left arm—these days the right one hangs inert at
his side—Germán Alcántara Carnero wraps his outsize
hand around the door handle and squeezes his long-
nailed fingers together, the rusted hinges creak as he
pulls, before ordering the dogs to stay. For the first time
in six years, the door swings open and in pour fresh air,
glimmering light, and all the warmth and aromas of the
Mesa Madre Buena. "Really, all I needed was to find out
how to connect with people . . . how to form *connections*,"
manwhoregrets says as he takes in what remains of the
garden. There is a mound of dry leaves under the fig tree,
pepper tree, and the cypress planted here many years ago
by Dolores Enriqueta in the hope that they would bring
her a healthy first child, and something rustling about
underneath—rats, he thinks it must be—but as the dogs
dash past him the leaves burst upwards and, with a great
clamor of wings, the blackbirds that were scratching
about for food in the leaves take to the air.

The blackbirds fly away, over a scattering of donkeys
and over the tops of the buzzing power lines that criss-
cross the mesa, away in the direction of the highway.
Watching the birds depart, birds that will again feature

at the end of this chapter, and watching the forms they trace in the air—a sphere, rippling waves, a braid, an elongated horn and a half-moon—he thinks of his own going away, and sees the farmland, the scrublands, the rocky outcrop, and the mountains as they were twenty years ago and not as they are now. "I won't stand a chance if I'm on my own . . . I won't make it the whole way . . . if I'm on my own solace will never be mine." No longer shielding his eyes, manwhoregrets is about to take a step but stops, placing his foot back down: "Really think this is the way . . . that it's other men you need . . . Really think they'd care . . . or that you could even make them listen . . . Why wouldn't the kingdom of heaven be enough for them?"

Yes, I do believe it, he thinks, picking up his left foot again and, having placed it forward, picking up his right. Then, turning, he puts the key in the lock without knowing why he does so—he doesn't plan on ever coming back—and turns once more and sets off in the direction of the scrublands. *Of course I believe it: they will come to understand that it isn't only heaven's solace they desire . . . when they hear my message they'll see they also want freedom here on earth . . . they will understand, and they'll join me, and together we'll walk the true path . . . one after another they'll enlist, they'll give form to the army I am founding this very day!* manwhoregrets says to himself, while also regretting the fact he did not set out like this years ago, when his body was not so worn out, when the sun did not weigh heavily on his back, when he could still remember how to address God's creatures and the manner to adopt if you want them to obey. Hurrying forward as best he can and hushing the six whining dogs at his heel, Germán Alcántara Carnero looks up at the horizon and sees the same flock again, forming cup and funnel-like shapes now—at the end of our story this flock will seem to form a huge turning windmill and then an immense blanket in the sky.

Laboring forward, manwhoregrets reaches to the last of the paths still visible on his land, the path used by the young girl who for the past five years he's paid to bring him food and to come and feed the dogs—the dogs now snuffling about their master, urging him on. "Of course I believe it: they will follow me on my path . . . I have found it and I will be the one to show other men . . . they'll *have to* follow my orders again today . . . all you need to do is find them, and speak to them . . . men who will form my army on earth!" ourman insists, coming to a promontory he would have had no trouble scaling thirty or forty years ago but that now is as good as a vertical cliff face to him. Toiling up, Germán Alcántara Carnero looks out across the land: "Look for some familiar shape . . . a shape that is human . . . the outline of the first person to join the army of believers." The six dogs—confused and agitated by their master's conduct as he stands muttering to himself—muttering, that is: "Show yourselves, do not hide from me"—bark, whine, and turn circles on the floor.

After a minute of this—whining, turning in circles, and getting no response—the dogs begin biting their master's pant legs, while he merely goes on with his questions: "Where are the inhabitants of this kingdom? Where are my soldiers this day . . . the army that will walk with me . . . troops in the universal battalion of solace!" The dogs, baying and tugging at their master's clothes, finally succeed in setting him walking once more: manwhoregrets comes slowly down the other side of the promontory, and sets out along the sun-petrified path once more, stone-dry for lack of rain. Running his fingers over his neck, which is also splashed with moles and with small red cracks and with a thousand greenish veins, manwhoregrets wipes the sweat from his dripping brow, and quickening his pace a little, or at least thinking he does, he covers another twenty meters, stops, hushes the dogs with a wave of his good arm, and clambers onto a rock. In the distance, very far from where we are, he discerns a number of possibly human silhouettes.

Standing atop the rock, manwhoregrets squints, eventually deducing that they are indeed human forms. "The first . . . they will be the first to hear the word . . . the first to have to obey me . . . they will be my first recruits!" He climbs carefully down from the rock, in spite of the great excitement that has suddenly taken hold of him, and whistles at his dogs—the dogs that have lived by his side these five years past and that have shared his solitude, time, and seclusion—before setting forward along the path once more. Ignoring his rusty bones, his wasted tendons, and his atrophied muscles, manwhoregrets succeeds now in moving a little more quickly and not only in telling himself he is doing so. An eighty-meter stretch brings him to the rocky outcrop, and once he is among the high boulders, sunlight no longer falls from the sky alone: it rebounds off the glasslike edges of the rocks and the exposed seams of bright iron where portions of rocks have been shorn away. The path brings him, and us, down to a sunken but brightly lit clearing, the boulder around it obscuring the view, which makes him nervous. Germán Alcántara Carnero whistles to the six dogs again and quickens his pace, while murmuring: "Eight believers to carve a path with me . . . who will help me spread the news of the Lord's great compassion . . . who will help me bring news of the one true path, which exists in the collective life." Deciding he cannot wait for the path to emerge from the rocks, and seeing one some two or three meters high with an edge he might scale, he clambers laboriously to the top.

The eight men are only eighty meters or so away now and Germán Alcántara Carnero's heart begins to pound: *Plus they look ready, almost completely prepared . . . they're even wearing uniforms, five of them at least*, and then says at the top of his voice: "Why are they armed . . . what do they need those weapons for . . . who are these eight men?" Catching the scent of the eight men now some sixty meters away from the clearing, ourman's dogs turn and begin barking at the horizon. "Quiet!" shouts manwhoregrets. *I ought to get down and go over to them . . . I don't want the dogs to put them off . . . maybe they haven't seen me yet.* What ourman does not know and still cannot imagine, is that the approaching men did see him and are on their way to find him, and have in fact already decided, whoever he might be, to have some fun at his expense. "Quiet!" shouts Germán Alcántara Carnero again, raising his good arm. None of the dogs obey, and he despairs—he does not want the people in the distance to go away—before losing his footing and then, swaying for a moment atop the rock, loses his balance completely and falls—his body crashing against the obsidian and basalt jags as he comes tumbling to the ground.

A couple of minutes have passed by the time man-whoregrets regains consciousness, as the dogs snuffle at him and lick his face—they have detected the scent of the people approaching, and their hackles are up. Ourman, coming round, makes an attempt to rise, but, confusingly, finds his body unwilling: all the strength has gone out of him. A short while later the eight men come into the clearing, and he calls out for their help, these would-be soldiers in the army he is to lead, an army to bring tidings of great neighborly compassion to the world. Unlike his dogs and unlike the man he was many years ago, Germán Alcántara Carnero feels entirely unsuspicious of their approach, and lying twisted on his front in the clearing—a clearing which, viewed from above, has a strange shape: like that of a horn or tusk, the tip of which resembles the barbed tip of an arrow—calls out for assistance, or tries to: all that comes from his mouth is a string of bloody saliva.

Two of the dogs yelp and fall to the ground, to laughter from the men, who have taken up position at the entrance to the clearing. The rest of the dogs try to get away, but they go down, too: the men, now shouting and whooping, have leveled their guns and shot the beasts down. Manwhoregrets, still lying on his front, fails to comprehend anything that is happening—what are the gunshots, why are his dogs going down around him—and neither does he understand it when the men come forward, turn him over, and lay him against the rock he fell from. One of them steps forward and gives him a backhander across the face—*Not this! Why do they not listen? He brings good news!* "I know the way to your salvation!" he says through bloody teeth. "Listen! I know the way for you to give up your fear and sadness . . . I know where you can find solace . . . listen, listen!" And it is less clear still to manwhoregrets why these laughing men—*what, laughing?*—taking a few steps back, pick up stones and begin hurling them at his body—*what?*—but he does feel regret, regret upon regret: in particular he regrets ever having believed that solace would be found in the company of men.

Soon, the sound in his ears of the men's departing footsteps, he asks mercy for his dog—he can hear one of them whining excruciatingly nearby. For a moment his body contracts very slightly, drawing imperceptibly back into itself, before expanding beyond the confines of the flesh. It is 12:16 on November 17, 1981, the hour when the blackbirds appear over the clearing and pour down onto the body of ourman, covering him like a blanket, before dispersing across the immeasurable mesa, a place that from this day on, and like the rest of the country once illuminated by the memorable moments in the life of Germán Alcántara Carnero, will belong to him and to the beings that walk beside him.

ABOUT THE AUTHOR

EMILIANO MONGE (Mexico City, 1978) studied Political Science at the Universidad Nacional Autónoma de México. His first short story collection, *Arrastrar esa sombra*, was published in 2008, followed by the novel *Morirse de memoria*; both were finalists for the Antonin Artaud Award. With a wide array of non-fiction essays, reportage, and book reviews, he has been an ongoing contributor to the Spanish newspaper *El País*, the Mexican newspaper *Reforma*, and prestigious magazines such as *Letras Libres* and *Gatopardo*. He is the two-time recipient of the Fondo Nacional para la Cultura y las Artes Conaculta award, and is now a member of the "Orden del Finnegans," a group of Spanish-language writers that gathers annually on Bloomsday in Dublin in honor of Joyce's *Ulysses*. In 2011, the Guadalajara International Book Fair chose him as one of the top 25 best-kept secrets in contemporary Latin American literature, and in 2013 he was awarded the Corte Inglés prize "Otros ámbitos, otras voces." He was also selected for "México20", a list of twenty important young Mexican authors chosen by The British Council, the Guadalajara International Book Fair, the Hay Festival, and Conaculta. *The Arid Sky* is his first book to be published in English translation.

ABOUT THE TRANSLATOR

THOMAS BUNSTEAD is a writer and translator based in East Sussex, England. He has translated some of the leading Spanish-language writers working today, including Agustín Fernández Mallo, Eduardo Halfon, Yuri Herrera, Enrique Vila-Matas, and Juan Villoro, and his own writing has appeared in publications such as > *kill author*, *The White Review*, and *The Times Literary Supplement*. He is an editor at the translation journal *In Other Words*. He can be found on Twitter at @_thom_bunn.